Ellwood Roberts

Lyrics of Quakerism

And other Poems

Ellwood Roberts

Lyrics of Quakerism
And other Poems

ISBN/EAN: 9783744786553

Printed in Europe, USA, Canada, Australia, Japan

Cover: Foto ©Andreas Hilbeck / pixelio.de

More available books at **www.hansebooks.com**

LYRICS OF QUAKERISM

AND

OTHER POEMS

BY

ELLWOOD ROBERTS

NORRISTOWN, PA.
MORGAN R. WILLS, PUBLISHER
1895

CONTENTS.

LIST OF POEMS.

SONGS OF LABOR.

COMMUNION WITH NATURE.

LOOKING BACKWARD.

SONGS OF SUMMER.

THE GOODNESS OF GOD.

MISCELLANEOUS.

THE PARTING WORD.

LIST OF ILLUSTRATIONS.

TO ALL

WHO BELIEVE IN THE

PRINCIPLE OF DIVINE ILLUMINATION,

NO MATTER WHAT

THEIR DENOMINATIONAL ASSOCIATIONS;

TO ALL

MEMBERS OF THE

SOCIETY OF FRIENDS,

IRRESPECTIVE OF DISTINCTIONS AS TO NAME ;

AND TO

LOVERS OF NATURE EVERYWHERE,

THIS VOLUME IS

EARNESTLY INSCRIBED.

Ellwood Roberts.

ACKNOWLEDGMENT.

The illustrations in this volume were all made expressly for "Lyrics of Quakerism," and with two exceptions are from photographs taken by Jesse G. Butterfield, of Norristown.

The view on the Wissahickon, page 111, is from a photograph by William H. Richardson, and the Schuylkill in Winter, page 245, from a photograph by Frank C. Parker. Messrs. Richardson and Parker both reside in Norristown.

The plates from which the illustrations were printed, were made by the Electro-Tint Engraving Company, 1306 Filbert street, Philadelphia.

PREFACE.

The poems which compose this volume speak for themselves.

They are of such a character as seems to me to require no lengthy preface or formal introduction of any kind to the reader.

I take it for granted that those into whose hands the book is likely to fall, are fully capable of understanding the principle of divine illumination, which is the topic of a number of them.

I assume, also, that the great majority of men and women who take an interest in intellectual culture, are susceptible to the charms of Nature, which, from early boyhood, have been a source of delight and consolation to me.

The poet is, in reality, an artist, who evolves from his fancies, his experience, and his observation of what he finds in the world around and within him, that which will interest, attract and instruct the reader.

He does this more or less skillfully and artistic-
ally, according to the measure of inspiration with
which he has been endowed, without which no very
satisfactory or durable results can be accomplished.

His finished work is intended to convey to others
an idea of what he has himself felt and seen, and he
must expect to abide by a judgment, as to his success,
which is founded on the truthfulness and complete-
ness of what he has done.

He attempts to execute with his pen what the
painter of landscapes, portraits, or what not, essays to
perform with his brush and colors—the object of each
being to offer a true and faithful, and, perhaps, pleasing picture of what is presented to his own consciousness.

In either case, the highest excellence is that
which appeals to the intellect and touches the hearts
of those whom he desires to reach. Without being
able to do this, neither can rightly merit nor reason-
ably expect the satisfaction of that "well done" which
is the highest reward of the conscientious worker.

The belief in an indwelling light or power is older
by many centuries than George Fox and William
Penn, who made it the foundation stone of the Friends,
or Quakers. Poets and prophets had given it cur-

rency for ages. Since their time, Pope has written of it as that which

> " Warms in the sun, refreshes in the breeze ;
> Glows in the stars and blossoms in the trees ;
> Lives through all life, extends through all extent :
> Spreads undivided, operates unspent."

Members among all denominations into which Christians are divided bear testimony to the universality of this power. The higher the intellectual and spiritual endowments of men and women, the more fully they are convinced of it. Jesus spoke of it when he said to those around him : " The kingdom of Heaven is within you." I believe that it is destined to be an essential element in the religion of the future.

A few of these poems have appeared in the " Norristown Herald," the " Friends' Intelligencer and Journal," and other periodicals, but by far the greater number of them are now in print for the first time. I earnestly and humbly commend them to all in whose inner consciousness they may awaken an echo—content if they shall convey to some who read them the same sense of human need and divine beneficence which has actuated me in writing them, making my task easy, and insuring an abundant reward for my labor.

I.

LYRICS OF QUAKERISM.

The one corner-stone of belief upon which the Society of Friends is built is the conviction that God does indeed communicate with each one of the spirits He has made, in a direct and living inbreathing of some measure of the breath of His own life; that He never leaves Himself without a witness in the heart, as well as in the surroundings of man; that the measure of light, life or grace thus given increases by obedience; and that, in order clearly to hear the Divine Voice speaking within us we need to be still; to be alone with Him, in the secret place of His presence; that all flesh should keep silence before Him.

CAROLINE E. STEPHEN.

AT GWYNEDD MEETING.

The busy hum of noisy mill
   Has ceased, the farmer's toils are o'er;
Across the brook, and up the hill,
   We take our quiet way, once more;
And pause where summer sunbeams fall
   Upon the building, old and plain,
In which, 'neath shade of oak-trees tall,
   To worship God, we meet again.

We pause a moment—turn to look
   On all the lovely landscape round;
The valley down beside the brook;
   The slope beyond, with orchards crowned.
We enter; here, at least, we find
   No place for fashion, show or pride.
What need of these?   A peaceful mind
   Is greater joy than all beside!

No lofty note of praise we hear,
    No swelling strains of music rise ;
We come in trustful love ; no fear
    Disturbs the calm that round us lies.
We love the faith our fathers taught,
    That we, in thoughtful silence, still
Must wait until God's hand has brought
    Our hearts submissive to His will.

The sunbeams flit across the floor,
    Blest emblems of that Love Divine
Which bids the sinful soul, once more
    Made whole by faith, in beauty shine !
The outward silence deeper lies,
    No motion stirs the summer air ;
We hear a voice at length arise—
        An earnest voice in solemn prayer :

" *Grant, Lord, that we may worship Thee*
    In spirit and in truth to-day.
Let every heart turn willingly
    To Thee, oh, Christ, the only Way !
An ever present Saviour, Thou,
    Teaching as never man has taught,
Oh, make us feel our weakness now,
        That we, without Thy strength, are naught !"

The words within our hearts abide
  As homeward bend our steps again,
With growing corn on either side,
  And fields of waving grass and grain.
Lord, may Thy presence, felt to-day,
  Be with us through the coming week ;
Recall our thoughts, so apt to stray,
  When paths prohibited they seek!

TIME'S VALUE.

How few there are who value time aright—
That treasure, given by the Infinite!
In youth we squander it, in age we grieve
At sight of loss we never may retrieve.
If you and I and all were truly wise,
The fleeting moments we would highly prize;
What sorrow and temptation would we shun,
How many good deeds do, now left undone!

DAWN, NOON, AND EVE.

Sweet is the dawn!
What hand can paint the glory of the morn,
The beauty of the East when Day is born?
The rich revealings of the Infinite
In every changeful ray of rosy light;
The wondrous glow that bids the world arise,
And see the miracle before it flies.
Oh, dawn is sweet!

So is life's morn
Beyond all other glory rich and rare.
The dewy freshness of the dawn is there;
The infant spirit thrills with pure delight,
As undreamed wonders burst upon the sight.
To be, to do, to know, have power to bless,
Things great and small, unnumbered charms possess,
In life's fresh morn.

Grand is the noon!
Midway between the morning and the night,
The earth rejoices in a flood of light.
How grand the splendor of the perfect day!
The sun has climbed the zenith on his way
To his far couch beyond the glowing West.
Morn is the time for labor ; noon for rest.
Oh, noon is grand!

So is life's noon!
Gone are the visions and the hopes of youth,
But in their stead the perfect light of truth ;
And though the wondrous loveliness of morn
Has passed, another glory has been born.
The rich perfection of the noontide hour
Brings full fruition of all strength and power.
Life's noon is grand!

Calm is the eve!
With its own beauty comes the close of day ;
The shadows lengthen all around our way.
In golden glory sinks the sun to rest
Within the glowing chambers of the West.
Day with its burdens and its toil is gone,
In solemn majesty the night comes on.
The eve is calm!

Calm is life's eve!
To those who have the heat and burden borne,
Of life's long day, faithful from early morn.
Their toil was sweet, the thought of rest is sweet;
They tread the downward way with willing feet;
The sun withdrawn, God's stars in glory shine;
Night, day—death, life—obey one law divine.
Life's eve is calm!

THE BRIGHTER SIDE.

Most men are full of joy when fate is kind
And when around them loving souls they find;
When shines the sun and all the skies are clear,
All hearts are full and overflow with cheer.

But when dark storms arise and cloud the sky,
And when unnumbered sorrows come to try
The spirit, shall it yield to grief and care?
Adversity's a test that few can bear.

A rule infallible, throughout the year,
We may apply, in clouds or weather clear;
'Tis this: Whate'er affliction shall be sent,
Look on its brighter side and be content.

NATURE'S TEACHING.

Wintry storms and summer showers,
  Lightning's flash and thunder's roll;
Song of bird and streamlet's murmur,
  Wake an echo in the soul.
Not a sight or sound is wasted,
  Not a note of discord dwells
In the grand, sweet psalm that ever
  From the heart of Nature swells.

Lo! around us and above us
  Sounds the summons everywhere;
In the ever-changing seasons
  Dwells a power that calls to prayer;
In the storm, and in the sunshine,
  In the gently-falling rain,
In the cloud, and in the tempest,
  Comes the message, clear and plain.

Forests clothed in regal beauty,
  Fields that wave with golden grain,
Skies suffused with sunset's purple,
  Flowers refreshed by summer rain;
Every breeze that sweeps the hillside,
  Every wave that laps the shore,
Every precious gift of Nature,
  Bids us worship and adore.

Who, unmoved, upon the glory
  Of the East can gaze at dawn?
Thoughtless, who can watch earth's waking
  From her sleep, when winter's gone?
Careless, who can hear the voices
  Of glad spring-time's jubilee?
See and hear, and yet unmindful
  Of their precious meaning be?

Overhead, when darkness gathers,
  Myriad worlds in beauty glow;
Hour by hour, the stars in splendor
  Beam upon the earth below.
Each, though voiceless, speaks in language
  Every heart can understand;
Supplements the day's glad chorus
  With a hymn complete and grand.

Earth and sea and sky invite us,
    Nature's myriad voices call,
Speak of truest praise and worship,
    To the heart in tune with all.
These I hear above, around me,
    As I look abroad to-day;
Nature's speech unto my spirit
        Seems, in plainest words, to say:

"Stand beside the mighty river,
    Rushing onward to the sea;
Linger in the forest's shadow,
    'Neath the leafy canopy;
Climb the high and rugged mountain
    Till the clouds encompass thee;
Go and look upon the ocean,
    Full of strength and majesty!

"Tell me, do the swelling murmurs
    Of the waters, as they roll,
Wake no echo in thy spirit,
    Stir no music in thy soul?
Can the branches wave above thee,
    And the birds around thee sing,
And no voice that bids thee worship,
    Through thy inmost being ring?

" Canst thou clamber into cloudland,
　Up the craggy mountain side,
Pausing here and there a moment,
　Gazing on the prospect wide—
Canst thou stand beside the ocean
　When the angry breakers roar,
Stand, and feel no impulse stirring,
　Teaching thee to bow, adore ?

" In the glowing face of Nature
　God's great love reflected see.
Lo ! the earth His presence-chamber
　Is, and evermore shall be.
Let, O man, His works so wondrous—
　River, mountain, forest, sea—
Teach thy spirit to acknowledge
　Him who speaks through these to thee."

TRUE HAPPINESS.

How shall true happiness be found?
    My neighbor's lands are rich and wide,
Kind Fortune pours her gifts around,
    His wealth is heaped on every side.
    His slightest wish is gratified,
His fertile fields with flocks abound,
    No blessing seems to him denied,
His praises through the land resound.
Yet, haunted by a vague unrest,
He feels he is not truly blest!

Can treasures vast, or broad estate,
    Can boundless honors, or a name
Inscribed with theirs whom men term great,
    And crown with laurel-wreaths of fame,
    Confer the boon?   Can loud acclaim,
Or any so-called gift of Fate
    Bestow it? art or science frame
A scheme whereby to reach the state
Of Happiness?   The wished-for prize
Which still, as man approaches, flies!

Ambition's restless fires may glow
　　Within the bosom ; hope of gain
May lure us onward ; beauty throw
　　Its spell upon the heart—in vain.
　　Blent strangely pleasure is with pain ;
Fate's stern decree has fixed it so.
　　Who would the crown of life attain
Must further seek, for this we know,
Each banquet has a spectre there—
Man's legacy of grief and care !

Men must forevermore aspire
　　Beyond mere trivial joys that pall
Upon their souls ; look upward, higher.
　　　　Past ages' voices to them call :
　　" Vain, empty pleasures are they all
That fill not up the soul's desire ;
　　Ye build your hopes on them, to fall
Before your eyes a ruin dire !
Such strivings ever must be vain,
Pursuit of pleasure ends in pain !

" Such joys no lasting peace afford,
　　The promised goal must still be won ;
Be wise, and seek the blest reward
　　In consciousness of duty done !

Go cheer the broken-hearted one,
Give to the poor from out your hoard,
  Do good from dawn to set of sun—
Sweet peace shall in your hearts be stored!
Who hath not this can never know
True bliss, for God hath fixed it so!

"A voice within you bids you turn
    From vanity and pride and show;
Refrain from evil still and learn
    The way that God would have you go.
    This is true happiness to know,
And well can man afford to spurn
    All knowledge that would have him throw
Aside such counsel, kind but stern,
Revealings of the Love Divine
Which ever round your pathway shine.

"There shall true happiness be found!
    The World may seem on you to smile,
And Fortune scatter favors round,
    Ambition lure you for awhile—
    Let not such songs your hearts beguile!
They are but vain and empty sound—
    The end lies further, many a mile.

These are not meant to be life's bound ;
They are but husks, that fill, indeed,
But do not satisfy your need.

"Why linger in a barren land ?
    Why longer in the shadows dwell?
The good ye seek is close at hand—
    God's voice within.   Oh, heed it well !
    Obeyed, its murmurs louder swell.
A guard and guide, behold it stand
    Beside you, prompt the way to tell,
Through wilderness or desert strand.
Its teachings heed, and it shall bless
With pure and perfect happiness !"

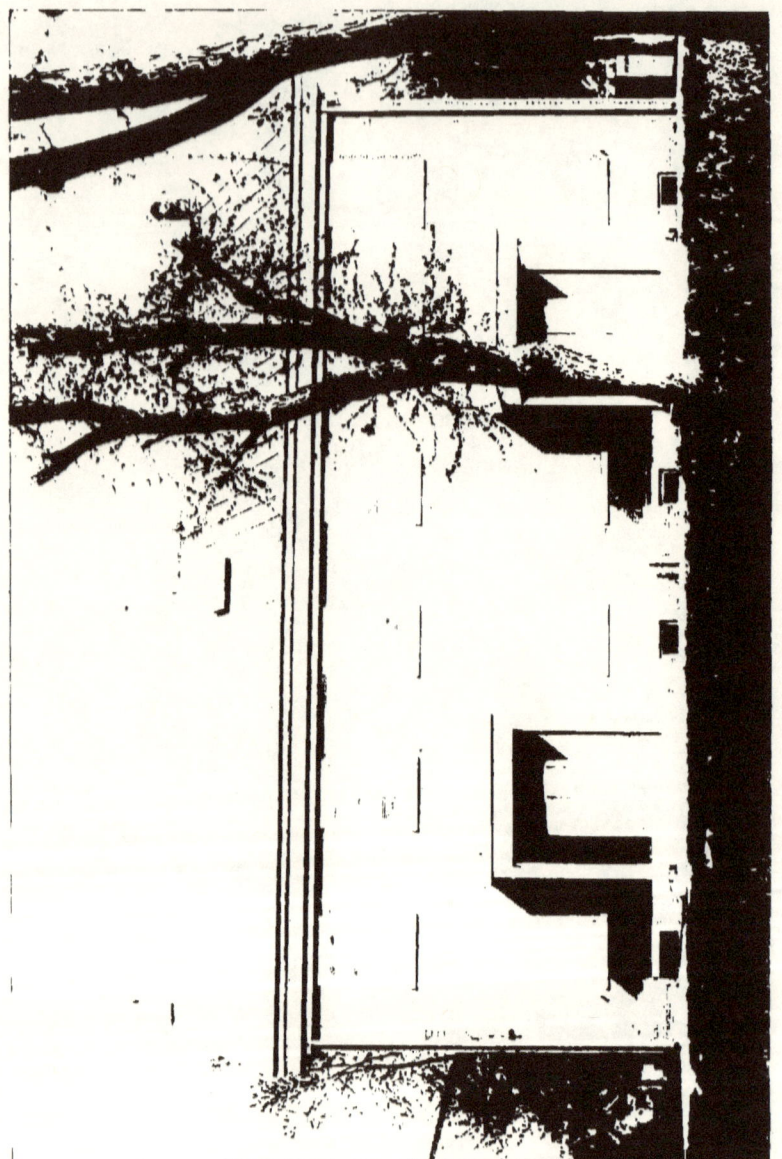

Norridge Friends' Meeting-House.

SILENT WORSHIP.

The summer sun is smiling down
Upon the hills of Norristown ;

To-day is Nature at her best,
In all the season's beauty drest ;

The Sabbath quiet in the air,
Itself a solemn call to prayer.

The church-bells ring from every tower,
We need no chime to mark the hour.

A small and silent company,
For worship gathered here, are we ;

Our recent losses we can trace,
See here and there a vacant place ;

The dead, we know, lived not in vain,
In recollection they remain.

May we who fill their seats to-day,
Be patient, just, and pure as they;

As full of zeal for righteous cause;
Like them, obeying Nature's laws;

As watchful, earnest and sincere,
In word, and deed, and worship here.

No organ peals, no swelling psalm
Disturbs the spirit's peaceful calm.

A still, small voice is sounding clear
To those inclined its tones to hear,

Who wait in quietness and peace
Until vexatious strivings cease.

In whirlwind not, or in the storm
God comes; we need no special form,

But eye to eye, and ear to ear,
We worship Him in silence here.

The stillness of all flesh we feel,
His message wait till He reveal.

Of gain or loss obtrudes no thought,
Each moment is with blessing fraught.

How hateful each besetting sin,
When tested by the Light within!

To hearts illumined by its ray,
The darkest night becomes as day;

Its warnings, slighted, are withdrawn,
Then gloom is ours although 'tis dawn.

How sweet such Love Divine appears,
With us abiding through the years;

It guards us, checks us, day by day
It goes before, and points the way;

It leads us, pleading tenderly,
That we may not forgetful be;

E'en through our inmost being thrills,
And all the soul with gladness fills;

Communes with us and bids us know
That peace which passes all below;

It speaks in power no human speech,
However eloquent, can reach;

Nor human learning, proud and vain,
With all its lofty flights, attain.

What need of any vocal word,
To us, our hearts so deeply stirred?

The manna which, like dew, distills
Upon the waiting spirit, fills,

To whom its precious treasures fall,
Hymn, sermon, benediction, all!

How vocal speech, in praise or prayer,
Would jar upon this peaceful air!

Each has its place; but now, instead,
A spiritual feast is spread.

The meeting ended, all bestow
A kindly greeting, ere they go;

A friendly pressure of the hand
That every heart can understand.

These over, slowly all depart,
That presence still within the heart.

Oh, may it linger all the day!
With bowed head to myself I say:

"A simple faith that knows no creed,
But turns to God in every need;

"As all the plants and flowers, we know,
Turn to the light, where'er they grow;

"So trusting hearts to Him are drawn
More often even than the dawn.

"No formal round of words may reach
The throne of grace; no artful speech

"Has power to call a blessing down,
Or worship with His favor crown;

"A God of love, abhorring sin,
His kingdom is the heart within."

We go, but long we feel the power
That dwelt around us for an hour,

Revealing more than wisest speech
From mortal lips could ever teach.

Who would not willingly abide
With such a teacher, satisfied?

The problem vast, from age to age
Perplexing prophet, priest and sage,

Is answered here—each soul within
A witness sure, rebuking sin.

The Light of worlds dwells not apart,
His temple is the human heart ;

And worship such as this to-day
In silent reverence we pay,

Accords more truly with His ways
Than long-drawn note of prayer or praise.

The meeting ended, all had re—
A kindly greeting on the way.—Page 44.

MAN'S IMMORTALITY.

How little that survives Time's touch we find!
　How much is lost, beyond all power to save!
We fear him, dread destroyer of mankind,
　Who levels proud and humble in the grave!

Wealth, rank and honors! these are but his spoil!
　Who glances at the ages past may see
How vain is strife, how unavailing toil,
　That seeks through these for immortality!

Kingdoms, republics, Time's mere playthings seem;
　They rise, a season flourish, then decay,
And yield, in turn, to others—like a dream
　These vanish too, as night succeeds the day.

Beauty is but a shadow in his sight;
　It lives a moment brief, and disappears;
Art, man and Nature! each is full of might,
　But none can stay the ravages of years!

What meaning has the lesson of the past
  For us who dwell upon the earth to-day?
What is there firm, enduring?   What shall last
  Beyond the power of Time to sweep away?

The generations, as they come and go,
  Repeat the query; full of hope and faith
The answer seek to find, the truth to know,
  Whereby mankind shall triumph over death.

The question, ever new and ever old—
  The problem of man's immortality—
Comes home to each in turn with force tenfold,
  When through the mystic veil they fain would see.

Vain is the effort; age succeeds to age,
  To distant planet though man turn his eye,
Or earth and his frail works his thought engage,
  The secret still beyond his grasp must lie.

The individual shall pass away,
  Return to dust, and yet the race remain;
And through the future eons, day by day,
  New triumphs win and to new heights attain.

The influence of a pure and blameless life
   Is never lost, but lasts forevermore ;
Ours is the ripened fruit of toil and strife,
   Inheritance of ages gone before.

The toiler dies ! his words and deeds shall live,
   Posterity to bless, and aid, and cheer,
Down the long line of far-off ages give
   New strength to virtue through the eternal year.

The blessing, vainly sought, around us lies ;
   The Heaven, that seems so distant, is within ;
And in the life beyond who gains the prize
   Must here and now the blessed race begin.

Is man immortal ? every human heart
   Must unto its own depths for answer turn,
And, in the silence of all flesh, apart,
   In secret there commune with God and learn.

To know Him ! this is life eternal, pure,
   Beyond all pleasure time or sense can give;
Sweet His rewards, His promises are sure ;
   Who knows Him not has scarce begun to live !

The life within and life beyond are one!
  Man's heritage is infinite, indeed!
Why should he fear—his earthly journey run—
  To trust the Power that knows his every need?

The Present and the Future, in His sight
  Who makes His light within the heart to shine,
Are one; and one to men the day and night,
  Safe in the panoply of Love Divine!

EVENING.

Sunset's crimson light has faded
   Slowly from the glowing West!
Comes a holy calm about us,
   Every voice is hushed to rest.

Brightly beams the moon above us,
   And the stars their vigil keep;
O'er the sky a few faint cloudlets,
   Bathed in silvery brightness, sweep.

All the day our eyes turn earthward,
   And we toil, and buy, and sell;
But amid the solemn stillness,
   Closing round, we seem to dwell

Farther from the fierce temptations
   That beset the souls of men;
Farther from the evil, nearer
   To the Life Divine, again.

Let us ask ourselves the questions,
  Ere we go to rest to-night—
Have we kept the path of duty?
  Have we done our work aright?

Did the Sentinel, unmindful
  Of the precept, " Watch and pray!"
Leave the door that keeps the Tempter
  From the soul, ajar, to-day?

With the cares of life around us,
  Any act unjust, untrue,
Any deed unkindness prompted,
  Have we done or sought to do?

Have the lips essayed to utter
  Bitter words in anger's heat,
In the moment of our weakness,
  Used the language of deceit?

There is need for such inquiry,
  What we think, and do, and say;
There is need for closely watching
  Heart, and hand, and tongue, each day.

That, amid the solemn quiet,
  As we soberly review
Every motive, every action,
  We may gather strength anew.

Thus, bewailing each transgression,
  We shall learn to find delight
In the narrow path of duty,
  Learn to live each day aright.

HUMAN PROGRESS.

The world is moving onward,
  Although the march is slow;
The gloom and doubt have vanished,
  Of ages long ago;
The olden superstitions,
  Men day by day outgrow.

That morn is surely coming—
  Its dawning none can stay—
When men shall spurn the darkness,
  And error cast away;
Truth's power, at last prevailing,
  Shall shine abroad that day.

Its light shall bless the nations,
  All hearts shall feel the glow,
Man unto man be dearer
  Than in the past, we know,
And God Himself be nearer
  His children here below.

THE INNER LIGHT.

As sun's bright rays to outward sight,
　　Illuming and transforming all,
To inner sense the Inner Light,
　　Whose beams upon the spirit fall.

Blest emanation from the Source
　　That formed the world and bade it run
Uncounted ages on its course,
　　Its wondrous journey round the sun!

Part of the great All-Soul that fills
　　Unnumbered worlds that round us shine,
Within our inmost being thrills,
　　And melts our souls with love divine.

Its fullest measure dwelt in Him,
　　The Christ, who taught in Galilee
Of God in man ; through ages dim
　　The glory of that life we see.

He raised the fallen ; comforted
  The poor and needy; all His power
He used in doing good ; He shed
  Rich blessing round Him every hour.

And His disciples now are they
  (No matter what their race or creed)
Who hear that Inner Voice, obey,
  And follow where the Light may lead.

God is a spirit ; who aspire
  To worship Him in truth to-day
Must feel His spiritual fire
  Burn all the chaff and dross away.

His fan is in His hand, and He
  Will purge and cleanse His threshing-floor ;
Each grain of wheat shall garnered be
  Within His spiritual store.

In mercy and not sacrifice
  He has delight ; no outward show
His chosen fast ; who self denies
  And waits on Him, His peace shall know.

His goodness fills the universe,
　In Him we live, in Him we move;
As they in Eden felt the curse,
　So we—estrangement from His love.

God's witness in the soul of man,
　The true communion 'tis to know,
Which has been since the world began,
　Unchanged, though ages come and go.

Its wondrous rays enlightened all
　The prophets of the ancient days;
Encompassed persecuting Saul,
　And changed his cursing into praise.

The still, small voice of Sinai's height,
　The flame by night, the cloud by day,
That guided Israel's hosts aright,
　Directs, enlightens, guards our way.

And unto every humble heart
　That knows its sweet illumining,
It will to-day fresh grace impart,
　A peace beyond all measure bring.

The manna in the wilderness—
That Israel fed—and its pure ray,
Are like in this, that each to bless
Must fresh from heaven be won each day.

Each day, each hour, the waiting mind
Must seek the one true source of light,
And thus its highest blessing find,
Thus learn to worship God aright.

Eye seeth not, nor ear hath heard,
The treasure that within is shown;
The beauty of the Inward Word
The spirit knows, and it alone.

Yea, more than sun to outward sight,
Illuming and transforming all,
The shining of the Inner Light
Whose beams upon the spirit fall.

Blest messenger of power that fills
Uncounted worlds that round us shine,
Its message through our being thrills,
And melts our souls with Love Divine.

A PSALM AT TWILIGHT

Gazing upon the miracle of Spring
  When twilight's holy calm around me fell,
To parting day I heard the robin sing
  A fond farewell.

Born of the beauty that around me lay,
  A psalm arose within my heart to Him
Who fills our cup of blessing, day by day,
  Full to the brim :

"Oh, Giver of all good! Oh, Infinite!
  How full of earnestness our hearts should be,
How consecrated in Thy holy sight,
  Our lives to Thee!

"The human heart! Thy chosen dwelling-place,
  How can it be to brooding ills a prey?
Shall wrong or evil leave a lasting trace
  On it, to-day?

"Oh, that we never might Thy love refuse,
    When far from Thee in solitude we dwell,
What can we gain?   Alas! how much we lose,
        No tongue can tell.

"The world is full of tribulation, still,
    Who follows it shall find his cares increase.
Teach us to turn to Thee, to do Thy will,
        For this is peace.

" Be with us as we toil in weakness long;
    The old put off, renewed our strength shall be,
Within our hearts a new and holy song
        Of praise to Thee.

"Great Giver of each good and perfect gift,
    Be Thou our morning hymn, our evening psalm!
Thy wondrous love our troubled souls shall lift
        To perfect calm!"

My psalm was done, the twilight hour had passed,
    But overhead the stars shone pure and bright;
My soul, all day with dark clouds overcast,
        Was filled with light.

Sweet Nature's beauty, that around me lay,
  The thoughts within my heart, the twilight hymn,
Had filled my cup of blessing, on my way,
    Full to the brim.

In harmony with that delightful scene
  A sweet and holy calm like magic spell
Renewed my spirit, and a peace serene
    Upon me fell.

LIFE A BOOK.

Life is a book, 'tis said, on whose blank pages
  A record fair or full of blots we trace ;
Each thought, each word, each act, to last thro' ages,
  Is stamped in characters none can efface.

How are we writing ? how this record keeping ?
  Each page shows gain or loss on that before.
If gain be ours we have no cause for weeping,
  Joy reigns ; but loss brings sorrow evermore.

THE REIGN OF PEACE.

The blessed day is coming,
    When war's mad strife shall end,
When all mankind together
    Shall dwell, as friend with friend ;
That happy day, O nations,
    Pray God He soon may send !

Too short is life for striving,
    Let peace its treasures yield ;
Too sacred life for wasting
    Upon the battle-field ;
Poor triumphs those which only
    Are won with sword and shield !

Amid the gloom and darkness
    Of ages long ago,
The wild, untutored savage

Struck, madly, blow for blow,
And man, in brutal blindness,
Thought every man a foe.

But now the light is dawning,
 The past is gone for aye,
New lessons man is learning
 Of love and peace to-day ;
War, with its thousand horrors,
 Must surely pass away.

No longer men are groping
 In shadow black as night,
No longer rules the dogma
 That might alone makes right ;
The shadow lifts, the nations
 Advance into the light.

No more shall cannon's rattle,
 Like earthquake, shake the land ;
No more shall mighty armies
 Fight blindly, hand to hand ;
No more fly death and ruin
 Abroad at war's command.

The blessed light is dawning,
  Oh, may it still increase!
And bring that day's glad coming,
  When war and strife shall cease;
When all mankind together
  Shall dwell in perfect peace.

THE DIVINE PRESENCE.

No vain and foolish thought be mine
    Of Deity who dwells, to-day,
    From all His creatures far away,
Beyond the worlds that round us shine—

Who sees unmoved our cares each hour,
    To whom we dare not come too near,
    To whom we bow in servile fear,
Because we dread His awful power.

His presence fills creation's round,
    In Him we live, and breathe, and move,
    We have our being in His love;
Who, then, dare set Him mete or bound?

This language, this alone, I hear
    From lowly flower, from mighty oak
    That bends beneath the tempest's stroke,
"God dwells not far, but very near."

LIFE'S VOYAGE.

A sea is life, whose toil and strife
 And storms, mankind must dare ;
Undaunted, brave each rolling wave,
 And even shipwreck bear.

While skies are bright, and breezes light,
 And tempests far away,
How apt are all to pleasure's call
 To listen, day by day.

They take their ease, and fail to seize
 Swift opportunity ;
With mirth and song they drift along,
 Nor rising storms they see.

Swift speeds away the blissful day,
 Without a thought of night,
When terrors dark, around their bark,
 May fill their souls with fright.

When, overhead, thick clouds are spread,
  And angry waters roll,
And fierce storms sweep across the deep,
  They lose their self-control.

They cease to strive, and onward drive,
  Abandoned to despair;
They hurry on until the dawn,
  A prey to grief and care.

The braver soul, though sorrows roll
  Upon him, will not weep;
Though, like a pall, dark shadows fall,
  His course, straight on, will keep.

Faith need not fail though fiercest gale
  Around, above him, roar;
Its fury done, the warm, bright sun
  Will cheer his way, once more.

Each trial past, he will, at last,
  Attain that harbor sure,
Where wind, nor tide, nor aught beside,
  Shall mar his peace secure.

ABINGTON.

They builded wisely who upreared,
  Beneath thy giant oak-trees' shade,
A place for worship such as this,
  And strongly its foundations laid.
Thy grove itself, oh, Abington !
  A temple fit where men might pray ;
A place to hold communion sweet
  With Nature's God, this summer day.

No weaklings, surely, they who come,
  Where strength and beauty join as here,
And fill the seats within these walls
  At meeting-time, throughout the year ;
But strong and sturdy, pure and true,
  Who gather often here should be ;
Aspiring, hopeful, helpful, they,
  With oaks like these for company.

Two centuries ago they came,
  Who planted here Truth's fruitful seed;
From hand-clasp close of Fox and Penn
  They brought no narrow, sordid creed.
They owned no power of man to bind
  The conscience, or the mind control;
They scorned all priestly arrogance,
  That claimed dominion of the soul.

Obedient to the Master, they
  His kingdom ever sought within;
His Light the only exorcist,
  To enter there and cast out sin.
A sturdy race, no compromise
  With wrong they ever made or sought;
They squared their actions by the truth—
  To it, their touchstone, all things brought.

As wide as earth their sympathies,
  Man's universal brotherhood
They taught; and in their steadfast lives
  Exemplified their love of good.
They came in trusting faith that He
  Who led them from the world away,
Would guard and guide them o'er the sea,
  And still be near them, night and day.

For generations yet to come
  Who, in their own brief turn, should dwell
Where they abode, they wrought, content ;
  They labored faithfully and well.
With sires so strong, and just, and true,
  And mothers earnest and sincere,
What priceless heritage descends
  To sons and daughters round me here !

What legacy could equal theirs—
  A sense devout of human need,
A love of truth that ne'er grew cold,
  And hearts that held no narrow creed.
They labored well and not in vain,
  They sowed in fruitful soil good seed ;
Were we as faithful we should reap
  A harvest bountiful, indeed.

They builded wisely who upreared,
  Beneath thy giant oak-trees' shade,
A place for worship such as this,
  And strongly its foundations laid.
They builded wisely, strong and well ;
  Oh, would that we were wise as they,
As full of zeal for righteous cause,
  As true and faithful in our day !

DO THINE OWN TASK!

Do thine own task, and be therewith content.—GOETHE.

Do thine own task; look not to left or right;
Toil on in faith, according to thy light!
Thy neighbor's work is not assigned to thee.
Do thine own task; therewith contented be!

Pay not much heed to others' blame or praise;
Let thy own conscience judge of all thy ways!
The path of duty is the one for all;
Who elsewhere walks, shall stumble oft and fall.

Use well thy time; let neither praise nor blame
Retard thy wise pursuit of lofty aim!
Each has his own appointed work to do,
And sweet reward it brings to toiler true.

Go forth unto the toil assigned to thee,
Resolved to do it, whatsoe'er it be!
And, active, earnest, true and faithful still,
Do thine own task; God's purposes fulfill!

THE TRUE QUAKER.

True Friend is he who stands for what is right,
  Who casts expedience from him away,
Who waits and watches for the Inner Light,
  And its monition follows, day by day.

Who thus is taught will evermore be found
  Forbearing all in charity and love;
In earnest courage must his soul abound,
  And true to this, he lives all strife above.

In living as in faith, he will adhere
  To what is always simple, pure and plain;
In every thought and every deed sincere,
  He need not pause his action to explain.

In all his dealings faithful, honest, just,
  Abhorring gain derived from any wrong,
He shuns no duty, violates no trust,
  Withholds from none what may to him belong.

No bigot he, but, tolerating all,
  What he demands from each, to each he gives;
And, liberal in all things, great and small,
  Subservient to none, in peace he lives.

In all his wishes moderate is he,
  Formality and fashion he ignores;
His rule in all things wise economy,
  He gives to charity from out his stores.

Concerned to live aright in every way,
  With perfect trust in God, he is content;
His faith goes with him, every hour and day,
  Whether on work or recreation bent.

Hypocrisy and cant he justly spurns,
  Sincerity and truth his rule each day;
Set forms of speech and phrases trite he learns
  To shun, as savoring of mere display.

So, hating evil, humbly doing well,
  The Christ in man his faith and hope profound,
At peace with all mankind, his deeds shall tell
  How faithful he throughout life's busy round.

WORDS FITLY SPOKEN.

Words fitly spoken—how they cheer
The heart depressed by doubt or fear!
Suggest new efforts for the right
And lead us onward to the light.
How full of balm and healing they
When Sorrow's shadows cross our way!
A ministry of helpful power
They shed around the darkest hour.

Words fitly spoken! human speech
Was made the human heart to reach.
Who touches hearts himself must know
The spirit's tender overflow;
Rightly what should be said, must say,
Not more, or less, or go astray
In wastes of words to lose the way,
And wander from the light of day.

Words fitly spoken—how they light
The pathway in the darkest night!
Renew the courage, point the way
Distinctly as a star's bright ray.
Plain, honest, earnest, strong and clear,
Straightforward, sober and sincere,
Such speech has wondrous power to cheer,
Though all around be dark and drear.

Words fitly spoken jewels are,
More bright than beam from sun or star;
More rich than treasure from afar ;
They work for good, and never mar.
Their gladness on the soul they fling,
And comfort to each heart they bring.
There is no jewel, rich or rare,
With which they do not well compare.

Words fitly spoken—fruit of gold
On silver pictures, wealth untold
Their message to the heart, indeed,
To which they come, in time of need.
God's angels! how they bless the way
And turn the darkness into day;
Refresh the weary, comfort all
Upon whose consciousness they fall.

Words fitly spoken touch the heart,
Fresh courage for all tasks impart,
Renew the will to do and dare,
Remove a mountain load of care,
Lift up the burdens all men bear
Who would in life's grand triumphs share.
They fill the soul with joy and peace,
And bid all selfish striving cease.

Words fitly spoken! all their weight
In vain we seek to estimate;
Their share in what mankind call fate,
Their influence on us, soon or late.
The potent spell they cast may change
From ill to good a whole life's range;
Drive from the spirit grim despair,
And fill the soul with helpful prayer.

Words fitly spoken—how they heal
The sorrow every heart must feel,
And blessed sympathy reveal!
Their message, tender, sweet and wise,
Bids buried hope and faith arise
And look beyond the cloudy skies.
A balm to spirit wounded sore,
Let them abide forevermore!

Words fitly spoken—joy they send
To stricken souls and sweet peace lend.
God bless the hearts that comprehend
The peace they give to distant friend.
And may His ministry divine
Repay tenfold such gift benign,
More prized than wealth from richest mine,
More precious far than oil or wine!

Words fitly spoken—may they cheer
All hearts depressed by doubt and fear!
Lead all in darkness to the light
And pierce the gloom of sorrow's night;
Fill every soul with perfect peace,
Bid all unworthy striving cease,
Drive from each spirit grief and care,
And fill the soul with praise and prayer!

In shade of buttonwoods and oaks,
The plain, old-fashioned building stands.—Page 79.

HORSHAM MEETING-HOUSE.

A pleasant picture greets my sight,
　　Around me here are fruitful lands ;
In shade of buttonwoods and oaks,
　　The plain, old-fashioned building stands.
The glories of the summer day
　　An earnest, solemn sermon preach ;
The trees, the ancient meeting-place,
　　To me a silent lesson teach.

A century has come and gone,
　　O'er generations gathered there
At quiet meeting-time, perchance,
　　To hear a sermon or a prayer.
They gathered, full of humble trust,
　　To worship Him so near to all ;
Believing that His love divine
　　On every waiting heart would fall.

Within these walls what words of balm
    To spirits wounded sore have come;
What earnest pleading for the right
    From lips once eloquent, now dumb!
Ah! who can measure all the good
    Wrought out through faithful service here,
Performed by whom the Spirit moved
    To speak the truth in accents clear.

How many earnest, thoughtful ones
    Who worshiped here have passed away,
In yonder graveyard, close at hand,
    Names carved on those low stones shall say.
They toiled and loved, were loved in turn,
    Rejoiced and sorrowed as we do;
Fulfilled life's mission, day by day,
    And ran their race, as we shall, too.

Here, searching, honored names I find,
    Descending still from sire to son,
Unto their light how faithful they,
    In peace they rest, their journey done.
They tilled the fields that round me lie,
    They reaped the harvest, year by year,
They yonder met at meeting-time,
    Together, now, the dead lie here.

Beneath the shadow of these trees,
A century old, to-day I stand,
And gaze upon the lovely scene,
A fruitful, joyous, smiling land.
The glories of the earth and sky
To me an earnest sermon preach;
The memories of the meeting-place
A silent, solemn lesson teach.

REJOICE TO-DAY!

It is a comely fashion to be glad,—
Joy is the grace we say to God.
               —JEAN INGELOW.

Rejoice to-day! Delay not till to-morrow!
  The world is full of brightness and of bloom;
Too short is life for unavailing sorrow—
      Cast off thy gloom!

What though the day be dark, the sky o'erclouded?
  Rejoice! for soon the storm shall pass away.
Look up! thy heart must not in gloom be shrouded.
      Rejoice to-day!

The earth rejoices, full of tender beauty;
  And why should man be prey to grief or care?
Be wisely glad; make cheerfulness a duty,
      A joyful prayer.

Be glad! no matter if the way be lonely,
  The sun shall cheer thee with its blessed ray;
Remember that thou hast the present only—
      Rejoice to-day!

TRUE RICHES.

Why all this toil for triumphs of an hour?
What though we wade in wealth or soar in fame?
Earth's highest station ends in " Here he lies,"
And "dust to dust" concludes her noblest song.

—YOUNG.

Why do we waste the most of life,
Careless of better things, in strife
For worldly riches? since we hold
By such brief tenure lands or gold.

All riches fail; Time can destroy
What men collect; they but enjoy
Their treasures for a season, till
Life's sacred purpose they fulfill.

What is there truly theirs to-day?
What is there men can take away?
They all are equal in the grave—
The rich and poor, the proud and brave.

Go, stand beside the bed of death,
The faint voice hear, the feeble breath;
Behold the sunken eye of him
For whom earth's scenes are growing dim.

And tell me, in this awful hour,
How much avails him wealth or power?
What value now have lands and gold,
Or all earth's treasures, bought and sold?

The longest life is short, indeed ;
A little satisfies our need.
Avoiding each deceitful snare,
Be this the burden of each prayer:

" May we our hearts to Thee resign,
Oh, Father!   Lo, at Mammon's shrine
We cannot bow and serve Thee ; let
Thy love be our rich portion yet !

" Be every idol overthrown,
That all may worship Thee alone,
In whom all tribulations cease,
In whom alone is perfect peace.

" Be with us.   What to us shall be
All worldly wealth or poverty,
If Thou art absent ?   Let us hear
And know Thy voice, and feel Thee near !"

II.
SONGS OF LABOR.

"Labor is worship!"—the robin is singing:
"Labor is worship!"—the wild bee is ringing.
Listen! that eloquent whisper upspringing,
  Speaks to thy soul from out Nature's heart.
From the dark cloud flows the life-giving shower;
From the rough soil comes the soft-breathing flower;
From the small insect the rich coral bower;
  Only man, in the plan, ever shrinks from his part.

Droop not, though shame, sin and anguish are round thee;
Bravely fling off the cold chain that hath bound thee;
Look on yon pure heaven smiling beyond thee;
  Rest not content in thy darkness—a clod.
Work for some good—be it ever so slowly;
Cherish some flower—be it ever so lowly.
Labor! all labor is noble and holy.
  Let thy great deeds be thy prayer to thy God!

FRANCES OSGOOD.

BE PATIENT!

Oh, all who labor, all who faint,
    Let Patience be your guiding star!
Look upward! let no weak complaint,
    The glory of endurance mar.
We have our own appointed work,
    From which we must not turn away.
Have patience, brothers! Dare we shirk
    The labor God requires to-day?

And ye who struggle for the right,
    Amid the carnival of wrong,
Be patient! See the dawning light,
    For which ye hoped and prayed so long.
If you would seek to save the land
    From folly, prejudice or crime,
With hopeful heart and willing hand,
    Toil on! toil on! in trust sublime.

Press on! press on! the world must rise,
  Redeemed from Error's blighting sway,
And those on whom the darkness lies,
  Must see the blessed light of day.
But oh, be patient! Work and pray!
  The seed we sow in tears shall spring,
And, as the season wears away,
  A harvest rich and glad shall bring.

Dear hearts, to whom the night is long,
  Who seem to see no dawning bright,
Be patient! truth is ever strong,
  Look up! the skies are full of light.
No haste in all that wide domain,
  No tumult there, nor any jar,
But patience, peace and beauty reign,
  Enthroned in every glowing star.

Oh, sons of labor, all who toil,
  In forge or field, on land or sea,
Who weld the iron, or till the soil,
  Be worthy of your destiny!
And all who wage unequal fight,
  In striving for humanity,
In doing battle for the right—
  The victor's crown your own shall be.

The dear warm-hearted Summer bides,
   Through wintry days all dark and drear,
The rending of the veil that hides
   The glory of the perfect year;
Content to know that ice and snow
   Reign but for a brief season; then,
That flowers will bloom, and harvests grow,
   And Earth be glad with life again.

Be patient! seasons come and go,
   The buds unfold, the leaves expand,
And slowly, surely, daily, grow,
   The flowers that brighten all the land.
The perfect fruit must ripen slow,
   Amid the sunshine and the rain;
We plow the soil, the seed we sow—
   Months pass, we reap the golden grain.

Look up, and labor for the right,
   Enduring, hoping, striving long;
But oh, be patient! truth is might,
   And sure its triumph over wrong.
Though fierce and wild the tempests blow,
   And deeper make the gloom of night,
The darkest hour of all we know,
   Is just before the dawn of light.

What seems to-day a hopeless fight,
 The weak ones striving with the strong,
If true we yet shall win; the right,
 'Twas never meant should yield to wrong.
God lives, as ever, and His ways,
 Misunderstood howe'er they be,
Are highest wisdom; let us raise
 Our eyes to Him, and clearly see.

Be patient! let His love descend
 Like dew upon your souls to-day,
Refresh your wasted strength, and lend
 New vigor for to-morrow's fray.
Life is a constant warfare; they
 Who hope to wear at last the crown,
Must bear their burden day by day,
 Nor ever seek to lay it down.

Be patient! God would have us so;
 And they who strive to run the race
Before them, full of patience, know
 In Him a safe abiding-place.
Have Hope! it hath the power to cheer;
 Have Faith, whatever woes befall!
Have Love, and triumph over fear!
 Have Patience—blessed sum of all!

THE FARMER.

Toiling early and toiling late,
 Toiling patiently, day by day ;
Joy and peace on the farmer wait,
 As he faithfully works away.

Plowing, planting, with steady hand,
 Singing cheerily, now and then ;
Spring awaking, o'er all the land,
 Makes of him the gladdest of men.

Turns he furrows where soon shall stand
 Bright green ranks of beautiful corn ;
Grand his mission, his life-work grand,
 Though his fingers with toil are worn.

Health is his, and contentment, too,
 For, fulfilling the grand design,
Treads he pathways to Nature true ;
 She rewards him with peace benign.

All his goings in harmony
    With her laws, she is ever kind,
Showers blessings upon him free—
    Strength of sinew, and peace of mind.

Where is merchant, or priest, or judge,
    Quite so happy as he, to-day?
Folly to call him a toiling drudge;
    Rare gifts cheer him upon his way.

History teems with the mighty deeds
    Done by hero on battle-plain;
Better serving the nation's needs,
    Toils the farmer, with might and main.

What cares he for the city's brawl,
    Pride and fashion, and lust of gold?
Wise enough to despise them all,
    He has treasures, indeed, untold.

Balmy breezes, and skies of blue,
    Verdant meadows, and valleys fair,
Sweet birds singing the long day through,
    Peace and blessedness everywhere.

Summer sunshine upon him lies,
   Waving harvests around him stand,
Fields are fruitful, and bright are skies,
   He is happiest in the land.

Autumn comes; in the early morn,
   Though the frost still whitens the ground,
See him husking the golden corn,
   Piling the yellow ears around.

Rich abundance his labors yield,
   Gifts in plenty around him pour—
Fruit from orchard, and crops from field,
   Gathered into his ample store.

Winter gives him the rest he needs,
   Then the longer evenings come;
By his fireside his book he reads,
   Warmth and comfort within his home.

Barn and barrack are filled with hay,
   Crib and garner o'erflow with corn;
Sweet content is his part by day,
   Sound and sweet is his sleep till morn.

Bread for the millions there must be,
    He must thrive, lest the city fall,
Stay and staff of the land is he,
    Work he must, for he feeds them all.

Other workers may come or go,
    Little matters it, here or there ;
Want and hunger the land will know,
    If the farmer forgets his share.

Give him honor that he deserves,
    Let no burden oppress, unjust ;
From his pathway he never swerves,
    He is worthy of highest trust.

Toiling early and toiling late,
    Toiling patiently, day by day ;
Joy and peace on his footsteps wait,
    As he faithfully works away.

WORK AWAY.

Work away! Oh, do not stand
    Idly all the precious day;
Labor is there for each hand
    That is willing. Work away!

Do not seek to shun thy part,
    Do not leave thy work undone;
Labor with a cheerful heart!
    Toil was meant for every one.

Work away! Thy toil shall make
    Earth a paradise for thee;
Sin and dark Remorse forsake
    Him who strives contentedly.

Work! Let not thy soul be dumb;
    Not by faith alone can be
All thy trials overcome,
    Peace and triumph won for thee.

Look about thee; there may be
　Some one toiling also near,
Whom a kindly word from thee
　Hath the blessed power to cheer.

Oh, the incense of thy prayer,
　Offering of a spirit free
From all selfish, sordid care,
　Grateful unto God must be.

Wouldst thou give the meaning true,
　To the words thy lips may say?
Rise, and show what faith can do
　For the toiler.　Work away!

Stir the soil; the idle weed
　Must not occupy thy land.
Stir the soil and sow the seed;
　Thou shalt reap a harvest grand.

Changing seasons come and go,
　Each its task appointed brings;
Blessings all from labor flow,
　Highest good from action springs.

Every noble effort tells,
    Naught of that is ever lost ;
Wondrous power in labor dwells ;
    Count not what the stroke may cost.

Work to elevate mankind,
    Fields there are to harvest white ;
Work in earnest, thou shalt find,
    Leads thee on from height to height.

Work away! Thy toil shall bless ;
    Indolence can naught bestow.
Work away! Through storm and stress,
    True contentment shalt thou know.

Ease and rest are not for thee,
    He who trusts in them is blind ;
Who would truly happy be,
    Must his peace in action find.

Noble souls in bygone age
    Wrought, unknown, unloved, for thee,
Left to thee a heritage,
    Boundless as the land and sea.

So must thou for those unborn,
  Pass the hard-won blessing down;
Work away, from early morn
  Till life's sun in peace goes down.

Seek not, then, to shun thy part,
  Leave no task of thine undone;
Willing hand and faithful heart
  Grandest victories have won.

What to thee the praise of man?
  Sure reward thy own shall be;
Honest toil is Nature's plan,
  She will bless and honor thee.

Work, and thou shalt e'er rejoice
  O'er the good thy toil has won,
Daily hear the Master's voice,
  Saying unto thee, " Well done!"

THE PATH OF DUTY.

There is a blest reward of matchless beauty,
    Of peace beyond all power of speech to tell,
For him who, faithful, does his simple duty,
        And does it well.

For every one some high and holy mission,
    Some work to do, some purpose to fulfill,
There is; this truth, whatever man's condition,
        Remaineth still.

How oft brave spirits, in positions lowly,
    Have toiled, unknown, uncared for, year by year;
Have labored, while the work went on so slowly,
        No end seemed near.

However poor, or weak, or low their station,
    They did not shrink from toil, nor shun their part.
Brave souls! the thought should offer consolation,
        To every heart.

They strove for truth, and sought to point the lowly,
   In darkness groping, to the blessed light;
They did their duty, and each cause unholy,
     Essayed to fight.

And so to-day the weak ones, only, falter,
   And count the cost of effort for the right;
What nobler gift to lay upon the altar
     Than deeds of might?

The world is full of sadness and of sorrow,
   And thousands tread the paths of sin and pain;
And those who toil for such, to-day, to-morrow,
     Toil not in vain.

True workmen they who never pause to murmur,
   Or doubt His wisdom who is over all;
Who sees the oak, tho' bent by storms, grow firmer,
     And heeds each call.

Earth in her marvelous and perfect beauty,
   Beneath the summer or the winter sun,
Chides all her children who neglect their duty,
     For tasks undone.

The bright stars too at night, so full of splendor,
   Reproof convey to each unfaithful heart,
And they no sympathetic glance or tender
     To such impart.

To rightly live is not to strive for pleasure,
   Forever mingled, more or less, with pain.
Why should men spend their days in seeking treasure
     That brings no gain?

Though duty's path may not be always pleasant
   To outward eye, be sure it will afford
To him who toils, unmindful of the present,
     A blest reward.

There is a wondrous joy in simple duty,
   A precious peace, reward of doing well;
That fills each true and faithful heart with beauty,
     No tongue can tell.

TOIL WAS MEANT FOR MAN.

The lot of man is labor,
　'Twas not decreed in vain;
The idle soul grows stagnant,
　A breeding-place for pain.
We must be up and doing,
　True happiness to gain.

Was never greater error,
　Than work a curse to deem—
How sad were man's condition,
　With naught to do but dream;
Thus brutes may be contented,
　Which know not reason's gleam.

But man, the crowning glory
　Of Nature's wondrous plan,
Was meant for noble action,
　When life he first began.
Let all, contented, labor,
　Since toil was meant for man.

III.

COMMUNION WITH NATURE.

To him who, in the love of Nature, holds
Communion with her visible forms, she speaks
A various language; for his gayer hours,
She has a voice of gladness, and a smile,
And eloquence of beauty, and she glides
Into his darker musings with a mild
And gentle sympathy that steals away
Their sharpness, ere he is aware.   When thoughts
Of the last bitter hour come like a blight
Over thy spirit, and sad images
Of the stern agony, and shroud, and pall,
And breathless darkness, and the narrow house,
Make thee to shudder, and grow sick at heart—
Go forth into the open sky, and list
To Nature's teaching.

WILLIAM CULLEN BRYANT.

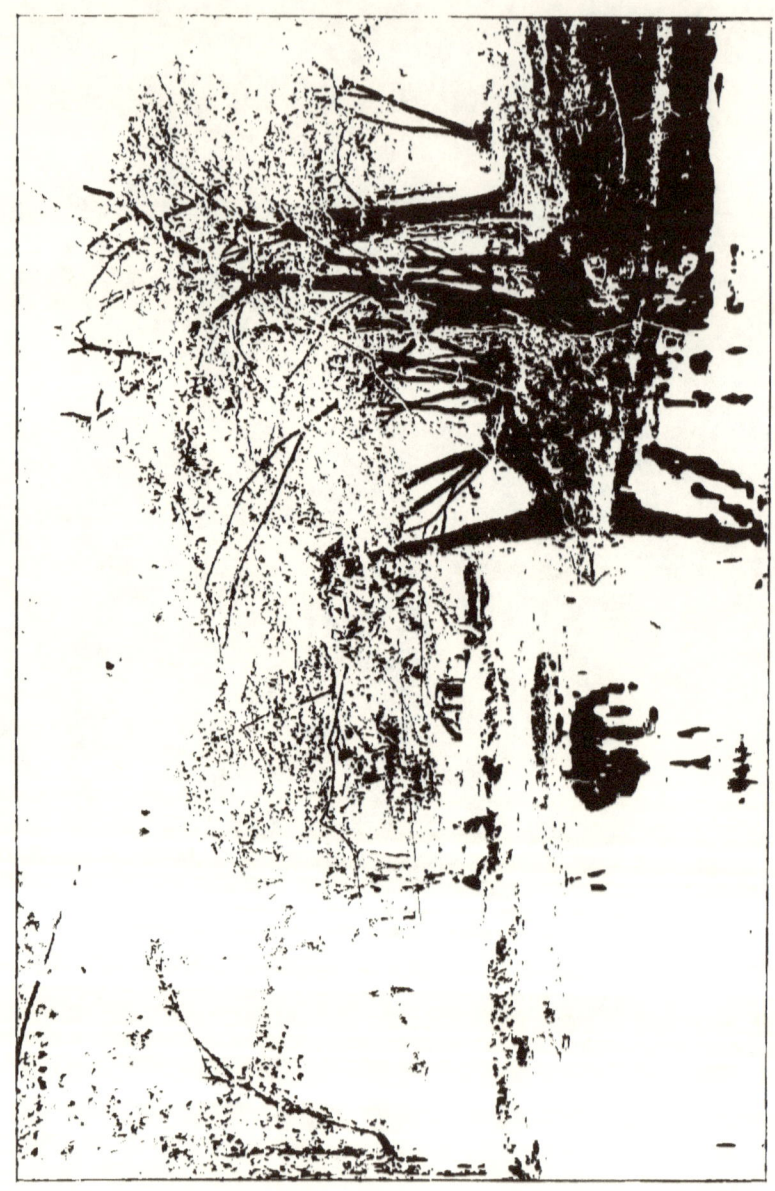

THE WISSAHICKON.

I sit beside thy bank, sweet stream,
  The summer sky above me glowing,
And watch thy waters brightly gleam,
  And hear the music of thy flowing.
Amid the season's beauties rare,
  Which every heart to new life quicken,
No spot on earth seems half so fair
  As thy sweet valley, Wissahickon!

The trees bend low above thy brink,
  Thy waters keep their green from fading;
The cattle come at noon to drink,
  Contented, in thy shallows wading.
When sultry heat is here, oh, stream!
  And hillside fields with drouth are stricken,
More beautiful than any dream
  Is thy moist vale, oh, Wissahickon!

The Indian dwelt upon thy shore,
　Before his steps the wild deer bounding;
He roams thy peaceful banks no more,
　Who gave thy name, so sweetly sounding.
Though, here and there thy forests grow,
　And on thy steeper hillsides thicken,
All else is changed except the flow
　Of thy bright waters, Wissahickon!

Thy current swept along in might
　To join the Schuylkill in its glory,
Long ages ere man saw the light—
　Compared with thine, how brief his story!
So, when the race has passed away,
　With final death and ruin stricken,
Thy floods shall roll upon their way,
　Just as to-day, oh, Wissahickon!

We change, but thou art still the same;
　From youth to age what quick transition!
We chase mere bubbles, wealth and fame,
　Lured on are we by fierce ambition.
But still thou flowest calmly on;
　Vain hopes that now our pulses quicken
Shall fail at last; when we are gone,
　Still shalt thou flow, oh, Wissahickon!

Thou art the fairest portion still
Of all the lovely scene before me.—Page 111.

I hear the locust's drowsy hum,
    The wild bee flits among the clover
Upon thy margin, where I come
    To rest, my week of labor over.
And here, till cooler breezes blow,
    And evening's shadows round me thicken,
I fain would sit and watch the flow
    Of thy bright waters, Wissahickon!

Now golden harvests crown the hill,
    And summer's loving sky bends o'er me;
Thou art the fairest portion, still,
    Of all the lovely scene before me.
When summer's light at last is gone,
    And all green things with frost are stricken,
How pleasant still to wander on
    Along thy banks, oh, Wissahickon!

Thy hillsides green are crowned with peace,
    And full of joy thy flowery meadows!
'Tis wise to let our wanderings cease
    In fond pursuit of fleeing shadows!
And to thy own sweet vale retire,
    Whose beauty every pulse must quicken;
The world has nothing better, higher,
    Than here we find, oh, Wissahickon!

Let others roam the wide world round,
    In search of wealth, or fame, or pleasure,
Contented here may I be found,
    My books, my toil, my home—my treasure.
And oh! may Fortune grant this boon
    To me when I with age am stricken,
To sit beneath the sky of June
    And hear thy murmurs, Wissahickon!

I pause within thy shade,
A brief hour here rest and refreshment find.—Page 113.

TO AN OAK TREE.

I pause within thy shade,
A brief hour here rest and refreshment find,
Beneath thy ample boughs, and call to mind
How often thus I've stayed.

How, in the first Spring days,
I watched thy swelling buds and listened long,
While some sweet bird poured forth a merry song,
A gladsome note of praise.

Thus at the rosy dawn
Of each bright morn I lingered—thus I knew,
Though the cold earth still wore her sombre hue,
That Winter must be gone.

And, later, when the heat
Of Summer hastened on, across my way
Thy shadow stretched, inviting me to stay,
And rest my weary feet.

Then would I musing lie,
And, gazing upward through thy canopy,
Sweet beauty in the passing cloudlets see,
That swept across the sky.

At morning and at noon,
Thy freshness and perfection make me feel
What wondrous charms kind Nature doth reveal
To hearts with her in tune!

And when long shadows fall
Across my pathway, and the night comes on;
When day with all its sights and sounds is gone,
Thy rustling leaves still call.

Thy strength and beauty blend
Most wondrously; for ornament and use
In thee so happily combined, produce
Creation's perfect end.

May we fulfill it, too!
For each is meant some noble destiny.
May we be strong and dignified like thee,
And to ourselves be true!

THE WOODS IN MAY.

There dwells a subtle fragrance
　Within the woods of May,
That baffles all description,
　Inviting us to stay.
Aroma of the spring-time,
　Of bursting buds it tells,
Of wild flowers bright unfolding
　From out their tiny cells.

The new-born leaves a tender
　And brilliant green display;
When come the heats of summer,
　It quickly flies away.
Among the trees we wander,
　With sense of keen delight;
We may not feel it later,
　Though sunshine be as bright.

Sweet Nature's resurrection
  From Winter's ice and snow,
Fills woods of May with beauty
  Beyond all else we know.
The fragrant honeysuckle,
  And dogwood flowers white,
Bloom here in all their glory,
  A vision of delight.

How natural to linger
  Among the woods of May,
So many wonders are there,
  Inviting us to stay.
Each bush and tree has treasures
  Of leaf, or bud, or flower;
No art there is like Nature's,
  When she exerts her power.

A tender, new-born glory,
  The leaflets all display,
There dwells a subtle fragrance
  Around our path to-day;
It bids us pause and linger,
  Ere it be gone for aye.
What joy and peace and sweetness
  Within the woods of May!

THE BIRDS OF EARLY SPRING.

Long before the grass is green,
When no flower or leaf is seen,
When the fields are brown and bare,
Bud nor blossom anywhere—
Come the happy birds to tell
O'er the tale we love so well.
Blessed messengers! they come
From their far-off winter home ;
Come, to tell us of the Spring,
Come, the tidings glad to bring
    Of the sunshine and the glory
    Of the long-expected Spring.

Through the long cold winter we
Sadly missed their melody ;
Missed the strains of music rare,
Such as fill to-day the air ;
Heard, instead, the North-wind high,
Arctic tempests whirling by ;

But we waited, day by day,
For the storms to pass away,
That the happy birds might sing
Their thanksgivings loud for Spring;
  For the overflowing sunshine,
  And the happiness of Spring.

Hear them warble!   Prophets they,
Heralds of a brighter day,
Full of faith they sing away,
"Gone, the winter's gone!" they say.
Hear them warble! everywhere,
On the earth, and in the air;
Every bush and every tree,
Vocal with their jubilee;
Not a note of sorrow there,
Not a trace of grief or care;
  Only songs of joy and gladness
  For the coming of the Spring.

Nature's minstrels! hear them tell
All the tale they know so well.
Lo! our hearts are touched to-day
By the simple words they say;
By their songs of joy and love,
All around us and above.

Creed and dogma men may teach,
Learnéd wisdom they may preach,
Higher than the heights they reach,
Is this gentle, simple speech.
Nearer, Father, unto Thee,
Listening, we seem to be,
    Hearing songs of sweet thanksgiving
    For the gladness of the Spring.

Happy creatures! while you sing
Of the beauty of the Spring,
Pouring forth a jubilee,
Full of richest melody,
Full of thankfulness and glee
For the sunshine, glad and free,
For the Father's loving care,
For His bounties, rich and rare—
Without knowing, you impart
Precious lessons, and my heart
    Blesses God for all the glory,
    All the joyousness of Spring.

Blessed songsters! may we know
Half the trusting faith you show;
Learn like you to find each day
Precious blessings round our way;

Learn our voices glad to raise,
Full of thankfulness and praise;
To express our gratitude
To the Giver of all good.
How can men forget to sing,
When your songs around them ring;
    Songs of praise unto the Father
    For the blessedness of Spring?

Blessed birds! oh, hear them sing!
Making all the welkin ring;
Perched upon a cedar now,
Or some leafless walnut bough,
Pouring out a jubilee,
Full of richest harmony;
Every note is free from care,
Telling of a future fair.
Filled with joy, oh, hear them sing
Their thanksgiving loud for Spring!
    For the wondrous joy and gladness,
    For the bliss that comes with Spring.

Nature's music! how it thrills,
Every heart with rapture fills!
Would that short and simple words—
Like the carols of the birds—

Every human heart might reach,
There abide, and something teach.
Songs, indeed, like theirs invite
Men to know the Infinite,
Trust His wisdom and His might
Who is goodness, love and light;
    Trust the universal Father,
    Whose the gladness of the Spring.

Happy songsters! let them sing
Praises of the blessed Spring.
Earth renews her youth each year,
Fields, now desolate and drear,
Green will be, and, round us here,
Summer's loveliness appear.
Nature, patient, bides her time,
Waiting for her glory's prime;
And the birds the secret know—
God, Himself, has taught them so;
    Taught them of the wondrous glory,
    And the gladsomeness of Spring.

Cheery minstrels! they have come
From their far-off Winter home,
Tidings sweet and glad to bring
Of the fast-approaching Spring.

What though ice and snow are seen!
They shall yield to Summer's green;
All the blessed birds foretell,
Joys outdoor we love so well.
We can trust the message clear
That, to-day, from them we hear;
Spring is coming, never fear,
Though the landscape yet be drear;
    For the birds have told the story
    Of the coming of the Spring.

God's own songsters! while you tell
Of the days we love so well,
Let our spirits make the tone
Of your music all their own.
It will banish grief and care,
Make the prospect doubly fair.
Lo! your trusting faith and love
Lift our souls all doubt above;
Tune our hearts to strains of praise
Unto God for bright Spring days;
    For the beauty, and the gladness,
    And the blessedness of Spring.

BLOSSOM-TIME.

The scent of apple-blossoms
   Is in the air to-day ;
Oh, say, why should we linger,
   When green fields call away ?
The streets are hot and dusty;
   Let us no longer stay.

The fields are full of beauty,
   The skies ablaze with light ;
The dewdrops on the clover
   Like diamonds gleam in sight,
And earth is kin to heaven,
   This morning fresh and bright.

Oh, blessed apple-blossoms !
   The sweetest time of all
Is when to field and orchard
   Your scent and beauty call ;
Who hesitates when bidden
   To such a festival ?

A MAY MORNING.

The mist of early morning
  Has slowly passed away,
A scene of rarest beauty
  Unfolds where late it lay.
What can surpass in sweetness
  The charm that dwells in May?

The wondrous fresh leaves glisten
  In sunshine glad and bright;
The birds, in merry humor,
  Give thanks for Spring's sweet light;
The miracle of May-time
  Bursts full upon the sight.

The whole green earth rejoices
  In warmth and light to-day;
The scent of myriad blossoms
  Is wafted far away.
Where is there other brightness
  Like that we find in May?

IV.
LOOKING BACKWARD.

My heart leaps up when I behold
  A rainbow in the sky :
So was it when my life began ;
So is it now I am a man ;
So be it when I shall grow old,
  Or let me die !
The Child is father of the Man ;
And I could wish my days to be
Bound each to each by natural piety.

WILLIAM WORDSWORTH.

The Old Schoolhouse.

THE OLD SCHOOLHOUSE.

Amid the trials of the changeful Present,
    The lights and shadows that around us play,
A retrospective glance is often pleasant,
        Along life's way.

In fancy once again youth's sunlight golden
    We feel; we tread the old delightful ways
We've trodden oft, while on the landscape olden
        We fondly gaze.

So down the well-remembered path I wander,
    Each step with some bright recollection fraught;
And all the changes, as I go, I ponder,
        That Time has wrought.

I reach the bridge and cross the sunny meadow,
    Ascend the slope, and, just beside the door,
The lofty chestnuts see; now in their shadow
        I stand, once more.

I enter, and behold, around, before me,
  Each once familiar object, as of old;
And, for a moment, I forget that o'er me
      Swift years have rolled.

A boy again, I strive to change the places
  Of Past and Present; for a moment seem
To live again amid the dear old faces,
      As in a dream.

Life's troubles, changes, toils, seem but a vision,
  As, sitting in the old, accustomed place,
Upon the world beyond, the fields Elysian,
      I turn my face.

How different reality from seeming,
  Since I have tasted what life had to give;
Can I have been for all these long years dreaming?
      Or, did I live?

The same, and yet how changed, the scene before me!
  The comrades of my youth have passed away;
I find myself—the thought comes stealing o'er me—
      Alone, to-day.

How few old friends survive the thousand changes
    Of half a lifetime! Thirty years have passed;
The mind down Time's long vista, busy ranges,
        With grief o'ercast.

The dear old friends have gone and left me lonely;
    Teachers and schoolmates—all have passed away;
Of most a recollection lingers only;
        Oh, where are they?

Alone! and all the eager aspiration
    I felt in bygone years, is mine no more;
I turn away in silent meditation,
        And leave the door.

I go my way, to present time returning,
    While sunset's fitful shadows hover near;
Within my heart the thought—I have been learning
        A lesson here.

We cannot feel again the sunlight golden,
    Although we tread the well-remembered ways;
We may not live again the moments olden
        In later days.

The years, in passing, break the spell that bound us;
No longer children, free from doubt and care;
New motives actuate, new scenes are round us,
Though not so fair.

Our hearts are changed; no more shall come the vision
That in the years of youth before us lay;
We may not hope to reach the fields Elysian,
Still far away.

THE OLD AND NEW YEAR.

The new year comes with silent tread,
  Its promise and its purpose vast ;
The old is numbered with the dead,
  The myriad ages of the past.
And, on the threshold of a year,
  We pause to pass in quick review
The record far and yet so near,
  Regret the old, and hail the new.

The solemn, changeless, distant past,
  And glowing, hopeful future, stand
Face unto face ; they meet at last,
  As heart to heart, and hand to hand.
The good and ill, the joy and woe,
  That marked the old year's rapid stride,
In swift remembrance come and go,
  Recede and swell, a changeful tide.

The fruitage that the past has borne,
　　We realize; our thought can trace
The deeds the past has wrought; we mourn
　　Because the wrong fills largest space.
But what is past for aye is done,
　　The mind, imbued with hope's sweet light,
Leaps forward.   Shall the year begun
　　Be crowned with triumphs pure and bright?

The closing year we fully know,
　　We trace its losses and its gain;
Oh, stranger, what shalt thou bestow
　　Of good or ill, of joy or pain?
Shall kindly feeling conquer hate?
　　And labor just rewards attain?
Or shall the land bewail the fate
　　That brings it want and woe again?

Oh, bright New Year! we hail thee now,
　　Thy months are full of promise vast;
Sweet hope is stamped upon thy brow;
　　May wrong be buried with the past!
May peace and plenty both abound,
　　May all mankind these blessings know;
And ages hence, the wide world round,
　　Men praise the gifts thou shalt bestow!

THE FARMHOUSE GARRET.

Afar from the city's dust and noise,
  Beside a grand old wood—
Away from the busy haunts of men—
  The ancient farmhouse stood.
By low hills girt was the well-tilled vale,
  A picture ever fair;
The fields were green and the skies were blue,
  And all was peaceful there.

A building quaint was that farmhouse old,
  In the days so long gone by,
And its dearest nook to us children all,
  The garret, strange and high.
The roof ran up to a peak above,
  The rafters all were bare,
No plaster covered the space between,
  We saw the shingles there.

Life then was new and the world unknown;
  A paradise to me
That garret old, with its treasures heaped,
  Its wonders, strange to see.
Its worn old books had a charm, indeed,
  I read them, hour by hour;
No stories like theirs I find to-day,
  Not one has half their power.

We children played in that garret old
  From noon till twilight fell;
To our young hearts it was fairy-land;
  How weird yet seems the spell!
Sometimes we heard on the roof outside,
  The pattering rain-drops fall;
But what cared we for the world beyond,
  To whom our play was all?

The hours flew swiftly, unheeded, by,
  And all too soon came night;
While there we mimicked the ways of men,
  With sense of keen delight.
The years fled fast, and the happy days
  Of childhood passed away;
Time came when we left the farmhouse old,
  And ended all our play.

From that wonder-land, so full of joy,
    Shut out, we scarce know how,
All, all is changed, and the mimic fun
    Is sober earnest, now.
The world and its ways familiar grown—
    Its marvels understood—
Recalled are days in the farmhouse spent,
    Beside the grand old wood.

The farm is sold and the house pulled down ;
    A mansion, stately, tall,
Stands now in place of the farmhouse old ;
    How changed, indeed, is all !
And they who played in the garret there,
    Are scattered, far away ;
So busy they with the cares of life,
    They rarely meet, to-day.

The fields are green and the skies are blue,
    The valley still is fair ;
The treasures heaped and the books are gone,
    There's none can tell me where.
Long years have passed, and I look in vain
    For what I used to see,—
When life was new, and the garret old
    Was all the world to me.

And, glancing back o'er the days of youth,
    I drop a silent tear
For the happy days, in the years gone by,
    Within that attic dear.
For sweetest still are the times long past,
    The faces gone for aye;
And Memory's treasures far outweigh
    All those we hold to-day.

CHILDHOOD'S DAYS.

When, glancing back to childhood,
  Its well-remembered dreams
Arise to recollection,
  How strange the survey seems!
How slowly passed the moments,
  The months were more like years;
And what provoked to laughter
  Becomes a cause for tears.

Then, living in the future,
  There was no cloud of care
Above the bright horizon,
  The prospect all was fair.
What structures then were builded
  By fancy every day!
Alas, how time, in passing,
  Has swept them all away!

And oh, what rude awaking
　　From dreams of days to be!
How different our visions
　　From life's reality!
No longer in the future
　　We live, but in the past;
So is the lot of mortals,
　　By strange ordaining cast.

How blissful all before us,
　　To childhood's hopeful mind,
When fancy roamed unhindered,
　　With no restraint to bind!
How long appeared the journey
　　Of life to youthful sight!
There seemed no bound or limit
　　To visions of delight.

The future all was sunshine,
　　No cloud obscured the skies;
There was no stormy weather
　　Beyond, to childish eyes.
The world, as then we saw it,
　　Was filled with noon-day light;
The days to come must surely,
　　We thought, be clear and bright.

Success the crown of glory
   In all our dreams attained,
Life's triumphs, as we saw them,
   Were all by merit gained.
To will was to accomplish,
   We could not comprehend
How lives that promise nobly,
   In utter failure end.

We erred in most things sadly,
   Our dreams of time to be
Were doomed to rude awaking,
   By stern reality.
Youth, careless, treads the pathway
   'Twere wiser far to shun;
By lessons sharp and painful,
   Its knowledge must be won.

Experience brings wisdom,
   And, looking back, to-day,
Upon the scenes of childhood—
   Retracing life's long way—
We see how slowly lessons
   Were learned that life has taught;
How small the room for boasting,
   In all that time has wrought.

Though some, perhaps, imagine,
　They, cheaply, good obtain ;
Amid life's busy turmoil,
　We pay for all we gain.
Our vaunted wisdom costs us
　Its worth, and often more ;
How many pay for knowledge,
　Its value, o'er and o'er !

What gain can make atonement
　For childhood's vanished days,
When all the future's glory
　Was spread before our gaze ?
What count our acquisitions,
　Our treasures, great or small ?
For childhood's joyous visions,
　Who would not give them all ?

MY BOYHOOD HOME.

There is no fairer spot on earth
    Than that dear place, my boyhood home ;
The fancies strange which there had birth,
    Remembered are, where'er I roam.
No other sunshine half so bright
    As that which gilded life's fair dawn ;
No other days so full of light
    As those of youth, forever gone.

I live those wondrous scenes of old
    In fancy often o'er again ;
Communion with the past I hold,
    Recall the pleasure and the pain.
The long sweet hours return to me,
    Just as of yore, where'er I roam ;
No matter where I dwell, I see
    No fairer spot than boyhood's home.

I wander far, but still I turn
  To that low roof which sheltered me;
For old beloved voices yearn,
  Although I know it can not be.
There is no spot the wide world round—
  No place I know, 'neath heaven's blue dome—
Where joy undimmed can e'er be found,
  Like that within my boyhood home.

No faces fair as those I knew
  In boyhood's days, now smile on me;
No flowers so gay, no skies so blue,
  No friends so true I ever see.
And when I wish for bliss complete,
  I turn my gaze (where'er I roam)
Upon those days, so long and sweet,
  I spent within my boyhood home.

No sunshine is there half so bright
  As that which gilded life's sweet dawn;
No days are half so full of light
  As those of youth, forever gone.
The fancies strange which then had birth,
  Remembered are, where'er I roam;
No spot so fair I find on earth
  As that dear place, my boyhood home.

AT FIFTY.

We glance, at fifty, backward more,
And forward less, than e'er before.
Spring days, with bud and bloom, are gone,
And glowing Summer hastens on.
The blessed harvest-time is here;
The ripened fruit of life's long year
Must soon, or nevermore, appear.
The sober Autumn-time is nigh,
And age's Winter, by and by,
Will come; we need not grieve or sigh,
For overhead is God's blue sky;
In hearts to Him and Nature true,
His peace abounds, the whole year through.

At fifty lovingly we gaze
Upon long-vanished childhood's days;
And dwell on those maturer years
Of early youth, their hopes and fears;
Live o'er again our manhood's prime,
When busy toil absorbed the time;
Almost-forgotten scenes recall,

When father, mother, home, were all;
Rehearse the long-unthought-of lore,
That dwells in memory's ample store.
The hours in reminiscence spent
Are filled with sense of calm content.

At fifty we have grown more wise
Than once we were; have learned to prize
The blessing that around us lies;
To seize each moment ere it flies.
The soul, intent on future bliss,
The good within its grasp may miss;
Ignore the present gift in haste
The sweets of coming joys to taste;
Forego the safer, surer gain,
For what it wishes to obtain.
The future is a world unknown,
The present moment ours alone,
And we can make it all our own.

At fifty we can estimate
Life's values at their own true rate;
Its joys so dear—unbought, unsold,
Which, none the less, are ours to hold;
The precious treasures we have found,
The circle of our firesides round,

By ties of sweet affection bound,
With virtue, truth and goodness crowned.
The blessings home and love bestow,
Are more than all on earth below.
Such riches evermore endure,
Who has them never can be poor.

At fifty we begin to look
At life as in an open book ;
Its pages carefully we scan,
To gather all the good we can.
With hearts too full for aught but praise
Of Heavenly goodness, now we gaze.
Behind us lies the tangled maze
Through which we trod in childhood's ways—
Before us Autumn's glorious days
Gleam on our sight through golden haze ;
While overhead is God's blue sky,
And round us Nature's glories lie.

At fifty doubts that once perplexed
The mind, are solved, and, all unvexed,
We scan the long half-century gone,
And trace our journey from its dawn—
As pilgrims, tired with hastening on
A weary circuit, clearly now,

From some high peak's unclouded brow,
Their wanderings far below can trace,
The paths they trod, from place to place.
How changed the prospect! all the scene—
From such a height—that lies between,
Is pleasing, tranquil, and serene.
Hills, groves, and fields of waving grain,
Blend in one vast and level plain.

At fifty much is yet to gain;
Who would the grandest heights attain,
Must follow paths of toil and pain—
Press upward ever, might and main;
Be thankful for the strength to shun
Temptation; for each triumph won;
The race before him, faithful, run,
And find content in duty done.
A mystery the human mind,
Where, intermixed with good, we find
The evils that afflict mankind.
But in each bosom glows a Light,
That, heeded, governs all aright,
And leads us on, from height to height.

At fifty we more clearly see
What once was wrapt in mystery.

We find no other thought so sweet—
No depth of gladness so complete—
As that which fills the soul secure
In its reward—a conscience pure.
Such treasures evermore endure ;
Without them, every one is poor,
E'en though possessing wealth untold,
Though blessed with boundless lands and gold.
Life's journey long indeed were vain,
Did we not learn this lesson plain.

At fifty, glancing back, to-day,
We marvel how, the whole long way,
The Light that guided early youth,
Has followed us—the lamp of truth.
How, when we heeded its pure ray,
The darkest night became as day.
Ignored, its warnings all were gone,
Then darkness reigned, from dawn to dawn.
God's Witness, lo ! its bright beams shine
On all who know its power divine.
A safeguard from all ill we find
Its tender impress on the mind ;
A presence that illumes and cheers
Through all the pathway of life's years.

FRIENDS OF OLD.

The friends of old! how true and tried,
  How dear ye are to me!
Were I to search the whole world wide,
  Your like I could not see.
What hand-clasp can with yours compare?
  What welcome gladder be?
Dear friends of old! what pleasures rare,
  You always bring to me!

Alas! I look around me here—
  Life's journey run so far—
How few of all I held so dear
  Left unto me there are!
The grave o'er some, for many a year,
  Has closed its portals dread;
Their voices I no longer hear—
  How silent are the dead!

And others now are scattered far,
  They come not back again;
In distant lands unloved they are,
  Their pathway marked with pain.
Dear friends of old! would ye were here,
  Your like I never see;
Your memory, still as ever dear,
  Alone remains to me.

Kind friends I find upon my way,
  Whose hearts are good and true;
Their presence cheers me, day by day,
  Their words my strength renew.
My soul with peace their hand-clasp fills,
  And in their eyes I see
Affection that my being thrills;
  How dear they are to me!

A friendly word, in time of need,
  Relieves the weight of care;
My pathway would be drear, indeed,
  Without the help they bear.
Their kindness I shall not forget;
  Close to my heart I hold
These friends of later life, but yet
  They are not friends of old.

Life's journey, though it be but brief,
  Outruns the friends of yore;
Time flies, and, like the falling leaf,
  They pass, to come no more.
Along the wayside, one by one,
  They fall, but I move on;
Almost alone, my course I run,
  The friends of old are gone.

Bereft of those I loved, I find
  The world grown strange and cold;
Gone are the faces, true and kind,
  The friends I knew of old.
The grave has closed its portals drear
  O'er most of them I know;
Their voices sweet I do not hear,
  As on my way I go.

And soon the last shall disappear,
  The friends of youthful days,
Who trod with me the paths so dear,
  The old familiar ways.
No wonder that I drop a tear
  For those no more I see;
Dear friends of old! would ye were near,
  This moment, unto me!

Dear friends of old! though most are gone,
  Beyond Death's soundless sea;
Hereafter, other shore upon,
  May we united be!
The end must come to you and me,
  Soon shall our course be run;
Dear friends of old! God grant that we
  May meet, when all is done!

YOUTH AND AGE.

The young look ever forward,
 And present good neglect;
The old glance ever backward,
 And on the past reflect;
These find in reminiscence
 The bliss which those expect.

But all along life's journey,
 From dawn until the night,
Are poured abundant blessings,
 To make the pathway bright;
The young and old may find them,
 If they but look aright.

Like sowing is the harvest
 That follows in its train;
Youth is the blessed seed-time,
 It never comes again;
For time that has been wasted,
 Regrets in age are vain.

HOME TIES.

Suggested by Thomas Hovenden's picture, "Breaking Home Ties.

A little world each household,
    Where all the loved ones meet ;
If kindly feeling govern,
    What happiness complete !
Along life's rugged pathway,
    Naught else is half so sweet.

The wealth of fond affection
    Is more than miser's hoard ;
Home ties and love of kindred
    The purest bliss afford ;
The acts by kindness prompted,
    Bring ever sure reward.

How blest are lives surrounded
    By love's sweet atmosphere !
Each spirit is exalted,
    And Heaven brought round us here.
Where kindly feeling governs,
    It gladdens all the year.

And those who spend their childhood
  Amid such scenes, look back
Thereon with wondrous fondness
  Throughout life's onward track ;
Of pleasant recollections,
  To them there is no lack.

And old home ties can never
  By any be forgot,
No matter where they wander,
  How rich or poor their lot ;
Their thoughts still turn forever
  Unto that sacred spot.

The home ties must be severed,
  They cannot always stay—
But dear the recollections
  That come, along life's way ;
They lead forever backward
  To childhood's far-off day.

THE GOOD OLD WAYS.

Who has not been disgusted oft
  Because of senseless change;
And rising indignation felt
  At fashions new and strange?
How much unlike the customs old
  Are those of modern days!
No wonder they sometimes complain,
  Who love the good old ways.

The men and women years ago,
  Were happy in their way;
They had their troubles, great and small,
  But not like ours to-day.
They came and went as pleased themselves,
  And gave but little care
To trifling matters such as vex
  And drive us to despair.

Decrees of fashion in their day,
  Were held in light esteem;
Just like their fathers did before,
  They floated down life's stream.
They viewed with more respect than we
  The customs of the past;
A race too slow were they, I own;
  May we not live too fast?

Each generation, we are told,
  Is wiser than the last;
We would not, if we could, recall
  The years forever past;
Where'er we go, from day to day,
  We find improvements vast;
And thankful we our lot on earth
  In such an age was cast.

But much we see, around us here,
  That merits little praise;
The simpler forms of speech are gone,
  The unaffected phrase.
Mankind love change; they lightly hold
  Bequests of former days,
Nor think how much of good they lose
  In leaving good old ways.

Some live, 'tis said, before their time,
   And others much too late;
Let not these last bewail the fact,
   Nor murmur at their fate;
For still we will to them concede—
   These changeful modern days—
That they must not be blamed because
   They love the good old ways.

CHILDHOOD'S DREAMS.

Youth's bright dreams linger with us yet,
  We trace them often, o'er and o'er;
Their charm we never can forget,
  While pleasure flows from memory's store.

Say not that childhood's dreams are vain,
  As waves that roll on ocean's tide—
That come and go, nor come again—
  As mirage on the desert wide.

What though they failed of being true,
  They served wise purpose, after all;
Part of our inner being grew,
  And there remain, whate'er befall.

The dream of childhood molds the man,
  Such inspiration has its power;
'Tis part of Nature's mystic plan,
  As seed brings forth the perfect flower.

V.

SONGS OF SUMMER.

I care not, Fortune, what you me deny—
  You can not rob me of free Nature's grace:
You can not shut the windows of the sky,
  Through which Aurora shows her brightening face;
  You can not bar my constant feet to trace
The woods and lawns, by living stream, at eve;
  Let health my nerves and finer fibers brace,
And I their toys to the great children leave:
Of Fancy, Reason, Virtue, naught can me bereave!
                                    JAMES THOMSON.

Tell me, what wants me here to work delight?
The simple air, the gentle warbling wind,
So calm, so cool, as nowhere else I find;
The grassy ground with dainty daisies dight,
The bramble bush, where birds of every kind
To waters' fall their tunes attemper right.
                                    EDMUND SPENSER.

THE STUDY OF NATURE.

Who studies Nature closely,
　A constant feast attends,
Which never palls or surfeits,
　But always pleasure lends;
Her ways are full of wisdom
　To one who comprehends.

The sky is full of beauty,
　The fields are ever fair—
Who gazes on the picture
　Forgets all selfish care;
At such a banquet table
　Are dainties, rich and rare.

One day the glories round us
　To field and forest call;
The next, the dark clouds gather,
　And rain, perchance, may fall;
Thus, endless alternation
　Makes glad the hearts of all.

Cloud, rain and blessed sunshine,
    Each in its turn we know;
How infinite the changes,
    In days that come and go!
Variety unceasing,
    And rightly ordered so.

We speak as though the seasons
    In all were only four,
But variation constant
    Prevails, the whole world o'er;
To-day is like no other,
    Its like may come no more.

So Nature works forever,
    To compass perfect ends;
Through sunshine, clouds and tempests,
    To one fixed purpose tends;
And all her ways are wisdom
    To him who comprehends.

A SUMMER RAIN.

For weeks the drouth had lasted—
　　The farmer's foe so dread—
The hillside fields were famished,
　　The grasses brown and dead;
The cornblades green were shriveled,
　　When shone the sun o'erhead.

The days were hot and sultry,
　　No cloud obscured the sun;
The nights were hot and dewless,
　　Of moisture was there none;
The streamlet in the meadow
　　Had almost ceased to run.

All Nature felt the pressure,
　　Each tender blade and leaf;
Her creatures all were silent,
　　As struck with sudden grief;
The earth looked up to heaven,
　　Imploring prompt relief.

At noon the bright sun dazzled,
    With fervent heat, the eye;
The hot air, rising, quivered
    Between the earth and sky;
Was never need the greater,
    Nor ever land so dry.

A south-wind rose at midday,
    More fiercely every hour
It blew, and still more fiercely,
    Disturbing leaf and flower;
It seemed the heat grew greater,
    And all things felt its power.

The maple leaves upturning,
    Predicted coming rain;
Such welcome portent never
    To grass, and corn, and grain;
Almost too great a blessing
    For thirsty hill and plain.

The dark clouds slowly gathered,
    The distant thunder rolled;
The play of vivid lightning,
    Of coming rain foretold.
The first drops came at nightfall,
    Worth all their weight in gold.

The long night through, the downpour
  Refreshed the thirsty land;
At morn the clouds, unbroken,
  Were piled on either hand;
All day the precious raindrops
  Supplied the sore demand.

An hour before the sunset,
  The dense clouds slowly cleared;
The rain at once ceased falling,
  The wind to west had veered;
And in the east a rainbow
  In glory now appeared.

Refreshed was every hillside,
  And grass, and corn, and grain,
Were clothed in freshest beauty,
  Because of blessed rain;
The earth looked up to heaven,
  In smiling joy again.

The miracle of moisture,
  Supplying Nature's need,
Her million-million children,
  No longer wretched, plead;
But all rejoice together,
  A happy brood, indeed.

Oh, dear rain-bringing south-wind,
Let Nature's anthems tell
The gladness of thy blowing
To fields that love thee well!
They thank thee for the blessings
That in the raindrops dwell.

JUNE.

Sweet month of June!
We would not have thee pass away too soon.
Thy long bright days are filled with pure delight,
And full of beauty every star-lit night.
Thy coming makes Spring's miracle complete
And perfect now, amid the Summer heat.
Field, forest, valley, hill, in splendor lie,
Beneath the glowing azure of thy sky.
The whole green earth is crowned with joy to-day,
Creation's myriad voices bid thee stay.
   Go not too soon!

   Thy balmy air
Is redolent of roses; beauty fills
The whole bright circle of the Summer hills;
The universe is like a harp that thrills
To touch of but one master; thou art he,
And the whole earth makes mighty jubilee.
Ten thousand voices, through the long months still,

Before thy advent, waken at thy will;
Now the grand chorus rises, night and day,
All pulses bound with life beneath thy sway;
All creatures strive to make amends, this hour,
For months of silence with their utmost power;
          This all their care.

          Who would not stay
Amid such loveliness as thine, oh, June?
The magic glory of thy splendid noon
Is all too brief, and fades its light too soon.
Who would not linger gazing on the scene?
The Earth is decked in bridal robes of green;
Her bridegroom is the Sun; his loving glance
Must all the beauty of her charms enhance;
And Nature hails the nuptial rites with glee.
Her children's voices sound a jubilee
          The livelong day.

          In the calm night,
The silent dews of heaven in peace distill;
Each tender blade of grass absorbs its fill,
Each is refreshed, in valley or on hill.
The gentle breezes stir the heated air,
And on their wings the scent of flowers bear—
Where harvests rich and glad and golden grow,

Make the wheat bend and rustle as they blow.
The night promotes abundance in its way,
It has its share in all, as well as day
    With sunbeams bright.

    Bid care begone!
When earth is bright with flowers, when roses bloom,
When floats on every breeze their soft perfume,
It is no time for sadness or for gloom.
When the whole universe is bathed in light,
Shall human hearts be clothed in shades of night?
When valley, hill-top, grove, with music ring,
Shall man, perverse, alone refuse to sing?
Shall doubt or gloom within his bosom dwell,
When lower creatures one glad chorus swell,
    From dawn to dawn?

    Day unto day,
And night to night repeat the tender strain,
Ten-million throats take up the glad refrain,
And tell the wondrous story o'er again,
With endless repetition.   Fruitful fields
Repeat it, in the plenty each one yields.
The orchard and the grove are gay with song,
All day; at night, the echoes linger long.
The mountains, clothed in grandeur, all rejoice,

The hills and vales awake and find a voice,
      Beneath thy sway.

      Glad month of June!
Thy days are bright with early Summer's light,
And witching beauty fills each star-lit night.
A thousand glories burst upon the sight,
Of those who wait and watch thy coming bright.
The miracle of Spring complete they see;
Thy advent fills the earth with melody.
The Schuylkill sweeps in flashing splendor by;
Beneath the wondrous glory of thy sky,
River and landscape, both in beauty lie.
We love the soft light of thy glowing noon,
We would not have thee pass, oh, blessed June!
      Away too soon.

The Schuylkill in Summer.

A MIDSUMMER DAY.

I.

MORNING.

The earth, aglow with beauty,
  Awakens with the dawn ;
How sweet the dewy freshness,
  Revealed when night is gone !
The bloom of bright midsummer
  On orchard, field and lawn.

In loveliness resplendent,
  The fields before me lie ;
A light breeze stirs the cornblades
  A moment, passing by ;
The sun, a blaze of glory,
  Ascends the glowing sky.

The morning, with its wonders,
  Is dear, indeed, to me ;
The hand of loving Father,
  In all things here I see ;
Than dawn, with dewy splendor,
  What hour can sweeter be?

The open air invites me,
  A thousand marvels call ;
On forest, field and river,
  The slanting sunbeams fall ;
The glad earth smiles to heaven,
  In thankfulness for all.

The charm of glad midsummer,
  Each bosom thrills to-day ;
It touches every object,
  At hand, or far away ;
Earth would be like to Eden,
  Could it forever stay.

The balmy air is laden
  With fragrant breath of flowers ;
The sense of Nature's wonders
  All other overpowers ;
Time passes, and too quickly,
  Are gone the gladsome hours.

Mid such transcendent beauty,
  No sordid thought can stay;
The heart is lifted skyward
  This blessed summer day;
And from our souls are driven
  All doubt and care away.

Rejecting pride and folly,
  Communion now we hold
With loving, kindly Nature,
  As man in days of old;
Ere yet the blight had fallen,
  The baleful lust of gold.

Her revelation teaches
  Of things unknown before;
For which is well forsaken
  That useless bookish lore,
Which makes him all the poorer
  Who has the greater store.

Who learns her lessons rightly,
  Transfigured is thereby;
His feet are on the greensward,
  His thoughts are in the sky;
Above each selfish impulse,
  His mind exalted high.

II.

NOONDAY.

The sun climbs higher, higher,
  The dew has dried away,
The light leaves scarcely rustle,
  So calm and still the day;
Unearthly now the brightness,
  Beneath the noontide ray.

No sign of gloom or shadow,
  On earth, in air or sky;
Upon the hillside yonder,
  The golden wheat-fields lie;
They tell to us the story
  Of harvest season nigh.

A light haze in the distance,
  Upon the landscape lies;
The far-off hills it softens,
  Their summits glorifies;
We gaze to grasp the brightness
  Of noontide ere it flies.

The sunshine gilds with glory
  Each object in our sight;
It falls upon the river,
  Before us flowing bright;
The surface that was silver
  Is golden in the light.

Noon's halo rich encircles
  The earth in brightness clear;
The hour crowns day with beauty—
  In such an atmosphere—
As rare and sweet midsummer
  With glory crowns the year.

The sun's rays fall directly
  Upon the earth below,
With force that tends to hasten
  The ripening process slow—
Grass, grain and fruit maturing
  That all around us grow.

So shall the harvest's plenty
  The husbandman reward;
His barns be filled completely
  With what his fields afford;
His only care to garner
  The gifts around him poured.

The circle of our vision
　　Is bathed in golden light;
The blue-domed sky above us,
　　Was never yet so bright;
A glamor rests this moment
　　On lowland, vale and height.

The glory of the dawning
　　Is wondrous fair to see,
So sweet the dewy freshness
　　Of sward, and plant, and tree;
The perfect noonday splendor
　　Is fairer still to me.

III.

AFTERNOON.

The sun has passed the zenith,
　　And, o'er the deep-blue sky,
The fleecy clouds are floating,
　　With idle motion, by;
So slow they scarce are moving,
　　Above the tree-tops high.

Gone, now, the shining luster
  Of noontide's dazzling glow ;
But river, field and forest,
  A perfect picture show
To one from hill-top gazing
  On all the vale below.

The shadows slowly lengthen,
  As midday glories wane ;
A softened light is falling
  On hill, and wood, and plain ;
Its mystic touch is resting
  On fields of waving grain.

A scene like this shall linger
  When years have sped away ;
The sweetest joy of summer,
  Is such a perfect day,
When Nature lies in beauty,
  Beneath the sun's bright ray.

The breeze that scarcely rustled
  The corn, an hour ago,
Sets every leaf a-quiver,
  In motion, to and fro ;
Each blade of grass is waving
  This way or that, below.

Sweet is the dewy freshness
  Of early morn to me;
But sweeter still the glory
  In noon's rich light I see;
The afternoon's soft splendor
  Is fairest of the three.

IV.

EVENING.

The long sweet day is closing,
  Its glories now are done;
A blaze of wondrous color—
  Although his race be run—
Behind the glowing hill-tops,
  In beauty sinks the sun.

The silent dew is falling,
  Grows cool the heated air;
The gentle winds of evening
  The scent of flowers bear;
Contentment, with the twilight,
  Is round us everywhere.

How changed is all in seeming,
  As twilight hour draws near;
The time for calm reflection
  And earnest thought is here;
In solemn silence round us,
  Acute the inward ear.

Close unto kindly Nature,
  All day, from early dawn,
We feel her precious presence,
  Although the day be gone;
Her charms exist as ever,
  The sun's bright rays withdrawn.

In eve a charm is present,
  That comes not with the day;
Peace reigns, as lengthened shadows
  Descend around our way;
To twilight hour belonging,
  With night it does not stay.

That day has wondrous splendor
  And grandeur all can tell;
But night has tender beauty,
  In which we love to dwell;
God rules the world of daylight,
  And rules the night as well.

The sky is bright and beaming,
　No clouds across it sweep ;
The moon and stars above us,
　Their silent vigil keep—
Their solemn watch incessant,
　The long hours, while we sleep.

The glory of the dawning,
　A miracle we call ;
So noonday's perfect splendor,
　And precious twilight's fall ;
The even, full of beauty,
　Is fairest of them all.

JULY.

Month of sultry noons and nights!
   Fields are parched for want of rain;
But thou hast thy own delights,
   Luscious fruits and golden grain.
Ripened wheat in heavy sheaves,
   Merry workmen store away,
Pile in barns above the eaves,
   On the mows of fragrant hay.

'Tis the bright noon of the year,
   Overhead the hot sun gleams,
Through the quivering atmosphere,
   Pierce all day his ardent beams.
Dewy night and misty morn
   Follow sunset bright and clear;
In the field the waving corn
   Sends aloft its stalk and ear.

Thunder-storms at midday rise,
　Veiling noon in deepest gloom,
O'er the clouds the lightning flies,
　How its flashes all illume!
Swiftly comes the dashing rain—
　Hillsides perishing with thirst,
Drink, and are refreshed again;
　Streams their limits quickly burst.

Gone the shower, the floods recede,
　Brightly shines the sun again;
Heat and moisture fill the need,
　Rich growth covers all the plain.
In the orchard apples show
　Rich tints borrowed from the sun;
Mid the bright green leaves they glow,
　Here and there a luscious one.

Month of sultry noons and nights!
　Fields are parched for lack of rain,
But thou hast thy rare delights,
　Sweet ripe fruits and golden grain.
Busy, languid harvest time,
　Days to Nature's lovers dear;
Summer yet is in her prime,
　And her glory crowns the year.

EARLY SUMMER.

Full of joy is early Summer,
  Growth and warmth and golden light;
Every day is crowned with beauty,
  Full of loveliness the night.
Dazzling sunshine brings the roses,
  Fills the whole bright world with bloom;
Day and night rejoice together,
  Banished now are doubt and gloom.

Skies serene and loving woo us
  To the woods and fields to-day ;
Who would linger long when Nature
  Calls him to her feast away ?
Earth a veritable Eden
  In the glowing sunlight gleams,
Life a grand and noble epic,
  Viewed from such a standpoint seems.

Gladness reigns the wide world over,
   Early Summer's golden light
Fills each bosom with thanksgiving
   For the season's blessings bright.
Happy harvest days are coming,
   Full of joy, throughout the land;
Where the fields of grain are waving,
   Full-eared wheat in shocks shall stand.

Perfect days that pass too quickly,
   One by one they come and go,
Each in turn reveals rare blessing,
   Beauty passing all below.
Balmy air and bright green landscape,
   Glowing eve and dewy dawn;
Sunlight's gold on field and forest—
   We shall grieve when these are gone.

Joyous time to him that loveth
   Growth and warmth and golden light;
Day is full of blessed beauty,
   Full of peace the dewy night.
Early Summer! time of roses,
   All the earth is filled with bloom;
Every heart in thee rejoices,
   Banished now are doubt and gloom.

AUGUST.

Now sober August comes—the scene,
  Beneath the Summer's sun still fair ;
The woods have changed their shade of green,
  New scents are floating on the air.
The farmer rests—the harvest o'er,
  Awhile from labor's steady strain ;
The season's crops are all in store,
  The barns well filled with hay and grain.

The Summer months are nearly past,
  Regretted much, they glide away,
And now we enter on the last ;
  A blessed trinity are they !
The lazy cattle in the shade
  Of friendly trees at noonday lie ;
Or, roused by swarming insects, wade
  In stream that passes murmuring by.

A parching drouth consumes the land,
    Deep lies the dust in all the roads,
How closely every cloud is scanned!
    The sultry heat a storm forebodes.
The rumbling thunder's warning sound,
    Faint in the distance now we hear,
With stifling air and thirsty ground,
    A welcome note it strikes the ear.

The storm comes on, the drouth is gone,
    Refreshing floods of rain descend;
All night it pours—another dawn
    Breaks slowly ere the showers end.
The drouth is gone, but with it all
    The glory of the Summer-time;
The leaves will soon begin to fall,
    The season now has passed its prime.

The tall corn, bending in the gale,
    The cooler night, the shortening day;
All Nature's voices tell the tale—
    The Summer passes soon away!
The fields of corn that ripen slow,
    Of Autumn speak, and breezes all,
That o'er the fields of stubble blow,
    Proclaim the coming of the Fall.

SONG OF THE CORN.

Have you seen a field of corn,
On an early August morn?
   Shine its leaves, all moist with dew!
How they glisten! How they gleam!
All the blades a-rustling seem;
Like to one who talks in dream,
   Thus they sing the whole day through:

"Now the happy hour is near,
When, upon each tall stalk here,
Shall a tiny shoot appear,
Which develops perfect ear;
With its bright grains, even, clear,
Rarest product of the year."

I have paused and seemed to hear,
In the rustling corn-song clear,
   Like a happy undertone,
Whisper, whether heard or dreamed,
Language very plain it seemed,
   Such as I had never known.

Says the rustling undertone:
" 'Twas for this, and this alone,
Giant stalks of ours have grown,
And their beauty here have shown—
Strength and loveliness their own.

" 'Twas for this in merry May,
That the seeds were hid away,
    In the earth—the grains of corn ;
Soon they sprouted, and a shoot
Sent straight up, and, down, a root,
    Strength and beauty thus were born.

"In the grain of corn a germ,
Safe from frost, untouched by worm—
    Lay, within the mellow earth.
Moisture, sunlight, warmth, were there,
Right the state of soil and air—
Each and all of them had share
    In the miracle of birth.

"Loving was the farmer's care,
Toiling all the long hours there,
    In the blazing glare of sun ;
Stirring soil, from day to day,
Pulling every weed away,

Lest it might the young growth stay,
Lest some injury be done.

" In the miracle of growth,
Gentle rain and sunshine, both,
Had their influence for good.
There had come, with days of June,
Dew of night and heat of noon ;
And the corn in beauty stood.

" It was left for hot July,
With its ever-glowing sky,
To perfect the growth you see.
While the sun its warm rays sent,
Frequent showers their moisture lent,
Force of fertile soil was spent—
Wonder-workers all the three.

" From the topmost blade, one dawn,
Ere the dew of night was gone,
Peeped the wondrous tassel down.
Soon the nodding plumes were seen,
Foam upon a sea of green—
Of all triumphs this the crown.

" Now the joyous time is near
When, upon each tall stalk here,

Shall in glory new appear
Tiny shoot that makes the ear ;
With its bright grains, even, clear,
Miracle of all the year."

Here the gentle breeze that blew,
Swelled a stormy gale into ;
And it swept across the field,
Making every cornblade yield.
Like sea waves, of tempest born,
Rose and fell the waving corn. ·

Now the gale, with shriek and moan,
Drowned the dreamy undertone
That I heard, or seemed to hear,
All along, in whisper clear.
It was lost in rustling roar,
Gone the note I knew before.

Surging, whirling sea of green !
What could all the tumult mean ?
Dancing, flying, up and down,
Still I saw the tassel's crown.
Stalk and blade in beauty there,
Never summer scene more fair !

Soon the fierce gale died away,
Calmer grew the August day.
Lower, lower still, it fell,
And the corn waves ceased to swell.
Then, succeeding harsh wind's moan,
Came the gentle rustling tone :

"Last month made the stalk complete,
Blade and joint and tassel neat ;
August, with its noontide heat,
And its cooler air at night,
Will develop—wondrous sight—
Husk, and silk, and perfect ear,
You can see them coming here.

"Come, and if you do not know,
I will tell you how they grow.
First, the tiny shoots appear,
They are coming, never fear,
For the hour is very near,
Yes, the earing-time is here.

"From the shoot in time will spread,
Bunch of long and silky thread ;
  When the gentle breeze shall blow,
On these filaments that rise,

Pollen from the tassel flies—
This the plan to fertilize
  Germs within the husk below.

"Thus the ear begins to grow;
In the husk are row on row
  Of the dainty shining grains.
All the night and all the day,
Dark or light, it finds a way,
Growing best when sun's bright ray,
  Monarch of the cornfield, reigns.

"Ripen soon the kernels bright,
Through the day and through the night,
  Harder growing very fast;
And when Autumn winds blow rude,
Yellow ears through husks protrude,
  Growth of corn is done at last!

"There the rusty blades are seen,
Shorn of all their tender green;
Soon the cutter's stalk-knife keen,
  Does its work among the corn.
Ranged in shocks the long rows stand,
Where the husker's nimble hand,
When the frost shall smite the land,
  Will his task begin some morn."

Whether heard I then, or dreamed,
Ask me not, but so it seemed,
  Sudden sob ran through the corn.
Was it fancy; who can tell?
Rustling leaves, as if there fell
On their undertone a spell,
  Silent paused a space to mourn.

But the sunlight's ray fell down
On each giant's tasseled crown;
  Stirred the gentle breeze again.
Through the field a tremor ran,
And the well-known voice began,
  Speaking then in language plain:

"Who has ever understood,
Who can measure all the good,
  Wrought by means of golden corn?
Wonder not I praise it here,
For the stalk and blade and ear
Furnish food the whole round year;
And without them, far and near,
  Man and beast alike would mourn.

"But my task is not complete;
Shocked the corn and gone the heat,
  Gone the Summer's wondrous prime;

There is something yet to tell
Ere we pause and say farewell,
   Comes the merry husking-time.

HUSKING-TIME.

"Merry husking-time! what joy
'Tis to happy farmer's boy!
Leaves have fallen, trees are bare,
Peace and plenty everywhere.
In the orchard apples rare
Hang from branches, here and there.

" Frosty are the fields at morn;
Hard and dry the grains of corn
Which in even rows appear,
Peeping from the yellow ear.
Skies are bright, and very clear
Is the autumn atmosphere.

" Huskers must not lie and dream,
Waiting for the sun's first gleam.
Long before the break of day
From their beds they rise; away
To their labor hurry they;
Theirs no time for pause or play.

" Tasks at barn and farmhouse done,
   Breakfast eaten as the sun
   Rises, and his beams appear,
   Through morn's hazy atmosphere—
   Promptly, to the cornfield near,
   Hie the huskers, full of cheer.

" Each unto his work must fly,
   See, the sun is rising high !
   Short the hours of daylight grow !
   Time is precious !   Down the row
   Of the rustling shocks they go ;
   Each upon the ground they throw.

" Prone on earth each giant lies,
   And his task each husker plies.
   Stalks are spread so evenly
   That the practiced eye may see
   Where to find the golden ear,
   Rarest product of the year.

" How the busy fingers fly,
   Seizing long stalks as they lie !
   Tearing withered husks away
   From the plump ears as they may ;
   Deftly breaking each with turn
   Of the hand that huskers learn.

" Grow the precious piles of corn
With the progress of the morn.
And the fodder on the ground,
Stalk and blades and husks around,
Into bundles huge are bound,
While the merry shouts resound.

" All the day the work goes on,
What was well begun at dawn,
Finished is ere sunlight's gone ;
To the barn the corn is drawn,
And the shining, precious hoard,
Safely in the crib is stored.

" Such a crop is wealth untold,
More than silver heaped, or gold.
Is it not to-day, indeed,
Miracle that fills such need ?
Man and beast alike would mourn
Were it not for golden corn."

Then the cornblades ceased to swell,
And the voice to whisper fell,
Solemn silence seemed to dwell,
There was nothing more to tell.
As the corn-song ended there—
Stalk and blade a picture rare—
Ne'er was summer scene so fair.

THE MORNING RAINBOW.

Eastern sky at dawn was bright,
　Glorious arose the sun ;
Everywhere was brilliant light—
　Day in beauty had begun.
But the West was overcast
　With a cloud, foreboding storm ;
Raindrops soon were falling fast,
　Then appeared the rainbow's form.

In the West, revealed to sight,
　Stood the arch of color rare,
Perfect in the glowing light,
　Yet a sign of sure storm there.
Rapidly the clouds o'erspread,
　Gone the wondrous rainbow bright,
Gone the fair sweet morn—instead,
　All around us gloom of night.

Came the warning not in vain,
    Gloom-enshrouded heavens frown—
Ere an hour had passed the rain
    Poured in dashing torrents down.
Through the long and gloomy day,
    Till the afternoon was gone,
Fell the rain from clouds of gray ;
    Such the end to perfect dawn !

With this day, in promise bright,
    Will some human lives compare ;
Perfect is the dawn of light,
    With a flush of color rare.
Bright the morn—too bright to last—
    Comes the cloud, and falls the rain ;
Soon is dawn's effulgence past,
    Early promise all in vain.

THE STORY OF THE WHEAT.

I.

NATURE'S SECRETS.

In the glowing light of June,
'Neath the bright-blue sky of noon,
  Waves across the wheat-field fly.
Breeze that scarcely stirs the air,
Sets in motion, everywhere,
Growing grain in beauty there.
Perfect picture! What so rare?
Never anything so fair,
  Underneath the summer sky.

Whence the wheat whose waves, to-day,
Form and break and roll away,
Never for a moment stay,
  Rise and fall, in rhythmic turn?
'Tis a secret Nature knows,
Which she can, alone, disclose.
Tiny seeds the farmer sows,

And the season comes and goes.
Mystic process! how it grows,
　　Seek in patience! you shall learn.

Who would Nature's secrets know,
Must be earnest; he must go
Unto her, for she will show
　　All to those who with her dwell.
Peace is with her, deep and wide;
Happy they who thus abide!
Unto them she will confide
Mysteries she has denied
Unto all the world beside;
　　All who know her love her well.

II.

PREPARING THE SOIL.

Well prepared the soil we see,
Plowed and harrowed, faithfully,
That the seed-bed perfect be,
　　Under early Autumn sun.
Where the precious seed shall lie,
Must be fertile, warm and dry,

Often—as the days roll by—
Stirred, that worthless weeds may die,
And no enemy be nigh.
    Comes a day when all is done.

Who would gather harvests grand,
Patiently must till his land,
Toil with brain, and toil with hand,
    Pausing never, long days through.
They that reap must rightly sow,
Days of anxious care must know,
Ere the crop in beauty grow ;
All good gifts from labor flow—
'Tis by Nature ordered so ;
    Nothing unto chance is due.

III.

SOWING THE SEED.

On September morning bright,
When the skies are full of light ;
Season, soil and weather right—
    Goes the farmer forth to sow.
Plump and clean his amber seed,
He has given special heed—

For of this he knows the need—
That there be no noxious weed,
Nothing harmful there, indeed;
   Lest the tares with wheat may grow.

Evenly he spreads the grain—
Not a cast of arm in vain—
All around him amber rain
Falls to earth to rise again;
   Here shall plenty's harvest stand.
Where he walks with steady stride,
Man and horse, and harrow wide,
Follow closely him; they hide
Precious germs, that shall abide
For a time, then, glorified,
   Rise to gladden all the land.

IV.

GERMINATION.

Now the grains are covered well;
Nature works her magic spell;
Change takes place in every cell—
   Mystic alchemy of growth!
From the base of embryo

Slender rootlets pass below ;
First, from central portion grow,
Then from either side they go—
    Heat and moisture aiding, both.

While the rootlets, left and right,
Downward pass, away from sight,
Upward, unto air and light,
    Pushes slender embryo.
And the growth proceeds so fast,
That, before a week is past,
Since the seed the farmer cast,
He who watches, sees at last
    O'er the field the young wheat show.

Colors varied first are seen,
Pink and purple, tender green,
And the shades that lie between—
    Beautiful, indeed, are they.
Fertile mold the rootlets feeds,
Well supplied the young plant's needs ;
Night and morn the growth proceeds ;
Glows the sunshine, falls the rain,
He who watches sees a gain,
    Steady, certain, every day.

V.

THE GROWTH OF AUTUMN.

Now the plants are multiplied,
At the foot the stalks divide,
Branching, often, far and wide,
　　Many there, where one before.
And, as Autumn days pass by,
Though white frost upon it lie,
Indicating Winter nigh;
Whether bright or cloudy sky,
Rainy day or weather dry,
　　All the ground is covered o'er.

Like a carpet is the mass,
Underfoot, as o'er you pass,
　　When you walk across the field.
Wonderful, that growth begun
'Neath the early Autumn sun,
Unto such a pitch should run;
Tangled triumph should have won,
Ere October's days are done!
　　Rich the far-off harvest's yield.

Chill November checks the growth,
Frozen ground and bleak wind, both,

Smite the plants to earth in fear.
But the tangled mass of wheat
Forms a blanket thick, complete,
Round the roots beneath your feet ;
In the stress of storm and sleet,
They will live though welcome heat
   Be denied through long months near.

VI.

PASSING THROUGH WINTER.

Winter comes, with clouds of gray,
Frozen is the earth all day ;
Shrinks the timid wheat away ;
   Darker now its hue of green.
Frost and thaw alternate reign,
But the firm roots of the grain
Its vitality maintain.
Though it make, no longer, gain,
It endures the stress and strain
   Of the icy storm-wind keen.

While the blasts of Winter blow,
Comes at length the welcome snow,
Mantle soft to wheat below—

Friend in hour of direst need.
Though the tempest rage at night,
Frost and Arctic wind unite,
Soon must each of these take flight.
Safe beneath its blanket white,
Waits the wheat till Spring's sweet light,
Wakes the earth to joy, indeed.

VII.

THE GROWTH OF SPRING.

Loosed at length is storm-king's hold,
O'er is tyrant reign of cold,
Comes the Spring, with joy untold,
　Melts the ice in sun's bright ray.
And the wheat-field, clear again,
Proves to us that not in vain
Lay the snow on hill and plain.
Now the welcome showers of rain
Bear rich blessing in their train,
　Growth is rapid, night and day.

April passes now away,
Comes the sunshine sweet of May,
Dawn and noon and eve, each day,

Full of peace and calm delight.
And the merry wheat, in glee,
Waves in every breeze; we see
How it joins the jubilee
Nature makes for sunlight free—
'Tis a kind of melody,
   Never ceasing, day or night.

Marvels new each morn appear;
Strength is needed for the ear,
With its weight of grain, and here,
   Jointed stalk, erect, we see.
Hollow column, it will bear
All the load that shall be there,
Nature's mechanism rare!
In the structure, all her care
That she may of waste beware;
   All is wise economy.

VIII.

THE EAR.

Soon the tender ear is seen,
Coming forth from tiny screen,
Backward rolls the blade of green,

And it stands in beauty there.
Crown of all is here at last,
Triumph of the long months past,
Since the seed to earth was cast.
Grand reward of patient toil ;
Product rare of seed and soil !
 Sun and rain had each their share.

Bearded spikelets, row on row,
To the very summit grow ;
Milky kernels each will show,
 When the time of bloom is past.
Sunlight sweet and showers of rain
Harden these to amber grain—
Hundred-fold has been the gain.
Waves in glory on the plain
Crop with plenty in its train,
 See it now matured at last.

Who would know it, late in June,
Under sweet midsummer's noon,
 For the tender plant he knew,
Months ago, ere winter drear,
Drifted snowy mantle here ?
Blade and stalk and well-filled ear
Perfect now do all appear,

In the noontide of the year.
Harvest-time is plainly near—
  Changed is green to yellow hue.

IX.

THE HARVEST.

Happy climax of the year,
Joyous harvest-time is here!
Season filled with Nature's cheer,
  Golden grain and ripe fruits rare.
Summer's glories overflow
Air above and earth below;
Everywhere its cheerful glow.
Fields are fair and skies are bright,
All is warmth and golden light,
Filled with beauty day and night.
  Joy is round us everywhere.

Falls the ripened wheat before
Reaper's steady stroke; no more
  Shall it wave in summer gale.
Heavy sheaves are quickly bound,
Placed in shocks the wide field round;
Firmly butted on the ground;

Capped, that sudden shower of rain
May not injure amber grain ;
All that has been done is vain,
  Now, if anxious care should fail.

When the sheaves are fully dry,
'Neath the sun of hot July,
  Safely they are stored away—
Precious sheaves, a whole year's bread !
In the barrack, barn, or shed,
Or on long poles overhead,
Packed in courses, they are spread,
Or, in careful order, laid
  On the mows of fragrant hay.

X.

THRESHING-TIME.

Ended well, task well begun !
Harvest over, all is done
Till, when gleams pale Winter's sun,
  Closing act has come at last.
Then, when Nature lies in sleep,
When the snow is drifted deep—
In the barn unwonted stir ;

Sheaves unbound, mid dust and whir,
O'er the spikes of cylinder,
     Through the thresher's maw are passed.

Winnowed clean from chaff and cheat,
Placed in sacks, the full-grained wheat
Is, indeed, reward complete
     For all toil and anxious care.
Since the day the seed was sown,
Many months away have flown.
Clouds have gathered, sun has shone ;
Rain has fallen, gales have blown ;
Changes of a year been known,
While the crop of wheat has grown.
     Wise ordaining everywhere.

XI.

TOIL BEFORE REWARD.

Man his blessings would not prize,
Did they fall, unwon, from skies ;
Labor all gifts sanctifies,
     Makes them ever seem more dear.
He who hopes to reap, must sow ;
Toil before reward must go ;

Without effort none may know
What this life was meant to show—
Sweetest joys of earth below.
He who makes the harvest grow,
In His wisdom fixed it so.
    This is true, the whole long year.

And the wheat whose waves to-day,
Form and break and roll away,
Underneath midsummer's ray,
    Teaches more than I can tell.
While with Nature we abide,
We are more than satisfied.
Nothing from us will she hide,
But reveal what is denied
Unto all the world beside.
Where is better, safer guide?
    All who know must love her well.

VI.
THE GOODNESS OF GOD.

Thou art the source and centre of all minds,
Their only point of rest, Eternal Word!
From Thee departing, they are lost, and rove
At random without honor, hope or peace.
From Thee is all that soothes the life of man,
His high endeavor, and his glad success,
His strength to suffer, and his will to serve.
But O! Thou bounteous giver of all good,
Thou art, of all Thy gifts, Thyself the crown!
Give what Thou canst, without Thee we are poor;
And with Thee rich, take what Thou wilt away.

WILLIAM COWPER.

THE GOODNESS OF GOD.

Who, gazing on earth in its beauty,
　　With sunshine and warmth all around,
With bloom on the trees in the orchard,
　　And carpet of green on the ground ;
Spring's gladness and peace the world over,
　　Sweet flowers bursting forth from the sod—
Say, who can behold without owning
　　The wonderful goodness of God ?

Who, watching June's marvelous splendor,
　　The miracles wrought by the sun,
The growth that leads up to the harvest,
　　Perfecting what Spring had begun ;
And, seeing such marvel, beholds it
　　Unmoved, or forgetful of Him
Who makes the earth glad with abundance,
　　And fills life's cup full to the brim ?

In changes that come with the Autumn
    His care and His watchfulness dwell,
And even the cold days of Winter
    The story unceasingly tell.
Though sunshine and warmth have departed,
    And deep lies the snow on the sod,
In Winter, as Summer, we plainly
    Discover the goodness of God.

All Nature unites in His praises,
    No voice that denies Him we hear.
We know that His goodness abideth,
    In sunshine and storm through the year.
With glance at the long months behind us,
    The devious paths we have trod,
Oh, how can we fail to acknowledge
    The wisdom and goodness of God?

The day, with its lights and its shadows,
    The night, with its darkness as well,
The dawn and the noon and the even,
    Of heavenly watchfulness tell.
Above us we trace the glad story,
    Within us we hear it again;
On the earth and the sky it is written
    Forever, in characters plain.

In seasons of joy and of gladness,
  To Him turns the heart that is true,
With thanks for the good He has given
  As freely as sunlight and dew.
Refreshing the souls of His children,
  His treasures unceasingly fall;
And vain are rejoicing and gladness,
  Unless He be present in all.

In moments of gloom and of sadness,
  When hearts are o'erflowing with grief,
We turn unto Him for assurance
  Of aid that will bring us relief.
When joy is our portion, we often,
  By folly and weakness beset,
Forsake Him; but, stricken with sorrow,
  His goodness we never forget.

Who scans Nature's face without reading
  This truth traced in letters of light—
The lesson of Heavenly Goodness—
  Sees nothing around him aright.
The breezes of night-time repeat it,
  The winds waft it over the sea,
And, deep in the heart, a soft whisper
  Reveals it to you and to me.

There's nothing, on earth or in heaven,
   But speaks of His goodness divine,
In language so plain, if we listen,
   We hear it, a message benign.
And none, glancing back on life's journey,
   Recalling the paths he has trod,
Can fail or refuse to acknowledge
   The wonderful goodness of God.

NEED OF DIVINE GUIDANCE.

In passing o'er life's pathway,
  How often, when we fall,
We know His aid extended,
  Who watches over all.
His care and loving kindness,
  How often has He shown!
Who trusts to Him shall never
  Be friendless or alone.

Who is there, glancing backward
  To youth, along life's way,
But must His power acknowledge,
  His goodness, every day?
He guided always rightly,
  He bade all doubtings cease;
And, where He led, no footstep
  But onward passed to peace.

And they who, willing, follow
   His guidance, all the day,
Need never pause or falter,
   Nor ever go astray.
They find that all their errors
   Are due to this alone:
His strength divine rejecting,
   And trusting to their own.

His children learn the lesson,
   Which all who live may heed:
That He is always near them,
   And knows their every need.
Without Him they must stumble,
   And often lose the way,
Because, to utter darkness,
   Is changed the light of day.

There gleams within each bosom
   A spark of love divine,
Which all who will may cherish,
   And let its bright ray shine.
Life's pathway must be gloomy
   And dark with clouds to all
Who shun this blessed guidance;
   They stumble oft and fall.

We need it night and morning,
 We need it all the day;
Without it, clouds and shadows
 Obscure the whole long way.
The sun may rise in beauty,
 His beams about us shine—
And yet we walk in darkness,
 Without the ray divine.

No good deed e'er accomplished,
 Along our pathway here,
But it was due to prompting
 Unto the inward ear.
The evil thought and action
 Are man's, and man's alone,
By selfishness suggested—
 The good is all His own.

We need His care and guidance
 In every act and thought;
His love is universal,
 With blessing ever fraught.
And wise are they who cherish
 The germ of love divine
That glows within each bosom—
 It will in glory shine.

His care and loving kindness
Surround us, day by day;
They guide and guard and cheer us,
Along life's toilsome way.
We must His power acknowledge,
His goodness we must own;
Who trust in Him shall never
Be friendless or alone.

OUR FATHER'S GIFTS.

How lavish our Heavenly Father,
  With bountiful gifts for us all!
He showers them freely upon us,
  About us each moment they fall.
They bless us from Life's early dawning,
  At morning, at noon, and at night;
All through the long year they attend us,
  Though stormy the weather, or bright.

Oh, how can we number them fully,
  Such treasures for you and for me!
Bestowed upon each of His creatures,
  So limitless, beautiful, free!
No end seems there unto the blessings
  And bounties that come to us all;
How thankfully hearts should be lifted
  To Him from whose fingers they fall!

For life and its many enjoyments,
  The senses with which we are blessed,
The health and the strength for such labor
  As gives to our living its zest;
For food, and for light, air and water,
  The talent and purpose to learn—
How can we sufficiently thank Him,
  Or render sufficient return?

For home and the bliss that it brings us,
  For loved ones, so dear to the heart,
For marvelous glories of Nature,
  For all the rich treasures of art.
Oh, how can we rise in the morning,
  Or how can we lie down at night,
Unmindful of these and all blessings,
  Though gloomy the season, or bright?

How lavish our Heavenly Father
  With treasures for you and for me!
They gladden our souls every instant,
  Poured out like the sands of the sea.
No step can we take but we find them,
  The gifts He intends for us all;
So freely bestowed on His creatures—
  About us each moment they fall.

Delightful the beauties of Nature,
　　The banquet prepared for us all;
Each month, what belongs to the season,
　　Is certain, howe'er it befall.
And we, looking on, must be mindful
　　Of Him, the great Ruler of all,
Whose beautiful gifts are the seasons,
　　The Winter, Spring, Summer and Fall.

The earth is His own and its fullness,
　　He rules it, by night as by day;
And man, if he follow best wisdom,
　　God's law in his heart will obey.
For, wonder of wonders, the Ruler
　　Of worlds without number, makes known
His Light in the souls of His children—
　　Not one of them journeys alone.

Approving the good, 'tis an angel
　　Of glory and blessing that leads;
Condemning the evil, it aids us
　　In weakness, revealing our needs.
In daylight and darkness it guides us
　　In safety, as long as we heed;
Withdrawn from us if we disdain it,
　　How gloomy our pathway, indeed!

How lavish our Heavenly Father,
With beautiful gifts for us all!
They gladden our hearts and assure us
Rich treasures, whatever befall.
Oh, how can we number them fully!
Poured out like the sands of the sea;
Bestowed upon every creature,
His bounty is boundless and free.

GOD IN THE SEASONS.

These as they change, Almighty Father! these
Are but the varied God.　The rolling year
Is full of Thee.—THOMSON.

Who watches all the changes
　Of seasons as they pass,
The bare, brown fields of Winter,
　The springing of the grass ;
The bud and bloom of flowers ;
　The heat of Summer days ;
The yellow leaf of Autumn,
　The Indian Summer's haze—

Must see that all is wisdom,
　That all God's laws are good,
And only that seems evil
　Which is not understood.
He dwells in Winter's tempest,
　As in the sunshine bright ;
His ways are ever wondrous,
　And all His doings right.

His goodness and His glory
  In everything appear;
He fills the earth with beauty,
  Throughout the whole glad year.
There is no gloomy prospect
  To those who trace His hand
Alike in field and forest,
  Alike on sea and land.

There is no height above Him,
  No depth He does not fill,
No space in earth or heaven
  In which He dwells not still.
We trace His wondrous presence
  In growth of blade and ear;
In every work of Nature,
  We see His hand appear.

And so we watch the changes
  Of seasons as they pass;
The bleak, bare fields of Winter,
  The springing of the grass;
The Summer's floods of sunshine;
  The Autumn's golden haze;
And thank God for His goodness,
  While learning Nature's ways.

VII.

MISCELLANEOUS.

Make yourselves nests of pleasant thoughts. None of us yet know, for none of us have been taught in early youth, what fairy palaces we may build; beautiful, proof against all adversity,—bright fancies, satisfied memories, noble histories, faithful sayings, treasure-houses of precious and restful thoughts.

JOHN RUSKIN.

Still waits kind Nature to impart
Her choicest gifts to such as gain
An entrance to her loving heart,
Through the sharp discipline of pain.

Forever from the hand that takes
One blessing from us others fall:
And, soon or late, our Father makes
His perfect recompense to all.

JOHN G. WHITTIER.

RIGHT AND WRONG.

A few short words, like grains of gold,
Sometimes a wealth of meaning hold ;
And some, though brief and simple they,
Are very difficult to say.

A learned man of long ago
Declared : " The hardest words I know
In all our language, short or long,
Are these—I own that I was wrong."

No kindly, gentle word we say,
Is ever lost or thrown away.
It wakes an echo to remain,
And gladden our own hearts again.

But oh ! the harsh and bitter taunt,
The cruel sneer, some soul may haunt ;
And, still remembered, linger long,
To testify that we were wrong.

We pass but once through life, we know;
A kindly action as we go,
The impress of a gentle tone,
Make glad all hearts beside our own.

We come not back to rectify
The errors made in passing by;
They must remain, however long,
Stern witnesses that we were wrong.

A daily record thus we trace,
A record nothing can efface;
For each unkind or loving word
That ever fell some bosom stirred—

Some warm heart filled with bitter woe
Or thrilled with pleasure's tingling glow.
Such things may be remembered long,
And stay to prove us in the wrong.

When, full of youthful ardor, we
First enter on life's work, we see
So much of evil in mankind,
That little to approve we find.

Unto ourselves we, musing, say:
We will attack and sweep away

The evils men have borne so long—
We mean to right at once each wrong.

But, as the seasons come and go,
And passing years their shadows throw,
We gather wisdom; in our kind
Much evil, but more good we find.

Where once we smiled, the warm tears start,
And tender pity fills the heart;
The task too great, the toil too long,
We sadly own that we were wrong.

Poor, restless mortals, we who stand
So near the silent, unknown land;
As seasons slowly glide away,
So we are passing, day by day.

A blameless record let us show,
A conscience clean and spotless know;
So at the end, though living long,
We need not feel that we were wrong.

AUSTIN L. TAGGART.

Built on the good old-fashioned plan,
He lived and died an honest man.
Faithful to every duty he—
Faithful, though all might recreant be!

Unmoved alike by praise or blame,
The title "Farmer," meant for shame—
The politician's jest—became
To him an honorable name.

Straightforward, fearless, on he went,
Upon the public welfare bent,
With conscience's "Well done," content;
His life is his best monument!

His motto, " Equitable laws,"
The common people's rights his cause.
He never faltered, knew no pause.

His voice, his vote, his blows of might
Were ever on the side of Right,
For Truth as he beheld its light.

Bowed down with grief we simply say:
"Would there were more such men to-day!"

DO THY WORK!

Do thy day's work
While yet the day is thine; before the light
Shall be withdrawn, and round thee settles night;
Life's day is short at best, and from its dawn
To oldest age a step—so quickly gone.
Toil on, with steady hand and earnest will,
Thou hast thy mission which thou must fulfill.
Let nothing tempt thee from thy task away,
For time is precious; and, while yet 'tis day,
No duty shirk!

Do thou thy part!
Remember, it is no disgrace to toil.
Go, weld the iron or cultivate the soil;
Or, better still, with hand, or brain, or pen,
Exert thyself to lift thy fellow-men
Above the common level, day by day;
But, still remember, as thou goest thy way,
The earnest worker triumphs, only he.
Who would achieve the highest good, must be
Forever watchful; all around us lurk
The foes that threaten ruin; go and work
With all thy heart!

Work with thy might,
And all thy might! Let nothing thee away
From chosen labor turn till close of day!
The calls of ease and pleasure thou must spurn,
If thou the blest reward of peace would earn.
Refuse to listen to the siren song
That lures thee from the right unto the wrong.
In honest labor ever safety find
From what may harm the body or the mind.
Deem it no hardship that thou toilest on,
Year after year, from morn till day is gone,
And cometh night.

From early dawn
Work on!   The day is thine, and blessed light
Shines round thy pathway; cometh soon the night.
Be earnest, active; make the most of life;
No crown he wears who falters in the strife.
And faithful service here alone can win
The high reward of living—peace within.
God loves the willing worker, He will cheer
Unselfish toiler through the livelong year;
Make thee rejoice as long as thou shalt live;
Assure thee treasure more than earth can give.
In faith toil on!

Th. Schuylkill in Winter.

JANUARY.

The short midwinter days are here,
　The nights are frosty now and chill—
The solemn midnight of the year—
　The snow lies deep on vale and hill.
No longer runs the streamlet nigh,
　The ice has bound its waters fast;
An Arctic wind is sweeping by,
　The bare trees shiver in the blast.

How changed the Schuylkill's tide! no more
　It sparkles in the noonday light;
The ice extends from shore to shore,
　Its strength increasing, day and night.
The skaters o'er its surface fly,
　In rhythmic motion, all the day,
While dark clouds sweep across the sky,
　Foreboding tempests on the way.

And soon we see the storm begin,
  All day the snowflakes scurry past,
All night we hear the tempest's din,
  The forests bend beneath the blast.
In whirling clouds the snow is hurled,
  Along the hillside, down the glen ;
Another day the whole bright world
  Is shut by drifts beyond our ken.

But soon the sun resumes his sway,
  His noontide beams are warm and bright ;
The stubborn ice-bridge yields by day,
  Though drear and sombre falls the night.
Alternate thaw and storm and cold,
  With snowdrifts deep and changeful sky,
The earth in chill embrace enfold—
  And so the month goes slowly by.

Midwinter days and nights so drear,
  With storm-clouds sweeping o'er the sky—
The solemn midnight of the year—
  Soon pass and leave no token nigh.
Bare trees that quake beneath the blast,
  Will yet be clothed in leafage bright,
And days so chill—the Winter past—
  Be bathed in floods of Spring-time light.

AT REST.

At rest; his feet shall tread no more life's highways,
  His eyes are closed in dreamless sleep to-day;
Others may wander in forbidden byways ;
  Our darling nevermore shall go astray.

At rest; the glad, bright world shall know him never
  Again who passes from its joy and pain ;
The being whom we loved has gone forever,
  But oh! what memories, sad and sweet, remain.

At rest; his soul was innocent sereneness ;
  Tho' young, he learned to give with generous hand.
So shall kind Nature deck his grave with greenness,
  When Spring-time wakes to beauty all the land.

Throughout the universe is compensation ;
  None perish utterly, none live in vain.
It may be, then (the thought is consolation),
  Our loss in him is balanced by our gain.

It may be other lives shall be completer
  Because of one whose stay was here so brief;
That sorrows shall be lightened, joys made sweeter,
  Thro' him, to those whose hearts are filled with grief.

They who have loved him, all their ties the dearer
  And closer now become, since he is gone,
May feel the tender spirit closer, nearer,
  Reflected from each face they look upon.

All, all must die; change is the fate of mortals ;
  But death must seem less dreadful in one home,
Since he has passed beyond the grave's dark portals,
  And gone where change or sorrow cannot come.

At rest; we take once more life's burdens sadly,
  And go about our daily tasks again.
He rests in peace; tho' storms rage ne'er so madly,
  He shall not be disturbed by woe or pain.

FEBRUARY DAYS.

The icy northern blast sweeps by,
  From wild wastes of the Arctic snow;
Above us droops a wintry sky,
  A bleak white landscape lies below.
But, 'neath the chilly Polar blast,
  A low, sweet undertone I hear:
"The wintry storms will soon be past,
  And pleasant Spring-time days are near."

In Winter's stern and icy grasp,
  Are river, pond, and rill, to-day;
Like iron bonds his fetters' clasp,
  Like despot's rule his frosty sway.
But only yesterday I heard—
  Though all the landscape was so drear—
The sweet voice of a lonesome bird:
  "The Spring-time days will soon be here."

The air is icy, keen and chill,
  All Nature lies in sleep profound,
That seems like death—so cold, so still—
  But flowers are biding underground.
The sun mounts up, from day to day,
  His beams each morn more full of cheer,
And to our hearts they seem to say:
  "The Spring-time days will soon be here."

The ice and snow will soon be gone,
  The Spring-time waits the sun's warm rays,
Already we can trace the dawn
  Of brighter, warmer, sweeter days.
Each morn we watch for signs of Spring,
  Each evening feel its coming near.
All Nature's voices seem to sing:
  "The Spring-time days will soon be here."

And though an Arctic wind sweeps by
  From wildest wastes of ice and snow,
And though above us wintry sky,
  And desolate white fields below—
Beneath the wind's wild organ-blast,
  A low, sweet undertone I hear:
"The wintry storms will soon be past,
  The sunny Spring-time days are near."

THANKSGIVING DAY.

Thanksgiving, blessed season! time to bind
  Closer than ever kindred's sacred ties;
To treasure friendships old, and new ones find,
  With thanks to God for all the gifts we prize!

The labors of the year are almost done,
  The crops are gathered, brown the fields, and bare;
Now feebly gleams the pale November sun,
  And Winter's frosty touch is in the air.

We have been blessed in basket and in store;
  What gifts to-day above all price we hold!
Peace that extends from shore to distant shore,
  Unnumbered treasures never bought with gold!

What nation, old or new, beneath the sun,
  Could celebrate Thanksgiving day as we?
What land has ever yet such triumphs won,
  As this, the happy country of the free?

We gather round the ample board to-day,
　　Acknowledging the Father's loving hand,
Whose bounties have been showered upon our way,
　　Whose benefits make glad the whole bright land.

Life has its trials, and each passing year
　　Takes treasures from us, bears some joy away;
Time brings its changes—vacant seats are here,
　　By loved ones filled on last Thanksgiving Day!

And so to-day we drop the silent tear,
　　Remembering those who from our midst are gone;
Recalling, too, God's mercies through the year,
　　Which, even in sorrow's night, have cheered us on.

No treasure can exceed a thankful mind,
　　A heart attuned to gratefulness and praise;
These more than ever let thy coming find,
　　Thanksgiving, best of all the holidays!

FORGIVENESS.

In human speech there is no harder word
To utter, though we know that we have erred,
Than this—forgive!   But who can turn away
From such a prayer, or lightly answer, " Nay" ?

Each human heart has sometime failed to show
That faithfulness to duty which we owe ;
And all, though proud or humble—all who live,
Have need sometimes to turn and say, " Forgive !"

The one whom I had loved and trusted long,
Yielding to sudden impulse, did me wrong ;
An enemy, indeed, may wound us sore,
But ah! a friend has power to injure more !

So bitter was the pain, so keen the smart
Of disappointment, that I lacked the heart
To stay and heap reproaches, to upbraid
The one who thus the debt of friendship paid.

And so, in silence musing gloomily,
Absorbed in thought, I stood, when slowly he,
In whom I thought each kindly impulse dead,
Approached; "Forgive me, if thou canst," he said.

How sudden was the change my feelings knew,
As all my own transgressions rose to view;
"Shall I, so prone to err, so apt to stray
From the straight pathway, not forgive to-day?"

'Tis brave to own a fault, in friend or foe,
The highest courage it requires, we know,
To say "Forgive"; then who can turn away
From such a prayer, or who can answer "Nay!"

As we forgive, the sweet thought comes anew,
As we forgive, we are forgiven, too;
Oh, may we learn the lesson, all who live
Have need sometimes to turn and say, "Forgive!"

MAY.

The happy birds trill forth a glad thanksgiving,
   Their voices ring throughout the livelong day;
At thy approach a sweeter joy in living,
     We feel, oh, May!

The opening buds, the wind so gently blowing,
   The golden sunshine and the flowers impart
New zest to life, and fill to overflowing
     The thankful heart.

We look abroad; we see the wheat-fields waving,
   The blossom-laden trees on every side;
Full seems our joy to-day; no restless craving
     Unsatisfied.

Up from the valley comes an echo pleasant,
   The music of the sweetly flowing rill;
Of all the links that bind the past and present,
     This brightest still.

We wait, oh, May! in Winter's storm and sadness,
Thy happy time, when trees are full of bloom;
When all the earth is hope and joy and gladness
And sweet perfume.

Amid the boundless glories of creation,
The wondrous miracles that round us shine;
Who fails to recognize the revelation
Of Love Divine,

Stamped in broad characters upon the pages
Of Nature's volume, fails therein to read
God's wisdom, still the same, through all the ages,
Is blind indeed.

And while we walk in silent meditation
Thy paths, oh, May, and all thy wonders see,
May we not fail to breathe the inspiration
That dwells in thee.

AN AUTUMN SONG.

The Summer's glories slowly fade,
  The fields in robes of richest green
Are clothed no more; on stalk and blade
  October's frosty touch is seen;
The landscape changes, hill and glade
  Look strange beneath the sky serene.

The leaves that once were green, are gold;
  Behold them falling, one by one!
The air is slowly growing cold,
  Though brightly shines October's sun;
What is it makes the earth so old?
  What subtle hand has mischief done?

The birds to other lands have flown,
  Save some poor wanderer, here and there,
Whose faint voice seems a wailing moan,
  So full of sorrow, grief, and care;
His mates have left him all alone,
  His burden more than he can bear.

How can he sit and gaily sing ?—
　Decay and ruin all around—
When falling leaves their shadows fling
　Upon him ere they touch the ground.
The season's changes sadness bring,
　It seems reflected in the sound.

He poured a song with joyous breath,
　When Spring's new wonders woke the earth;
How can he sing at Nature's death?
　The first to usher in her birth.
Too much for even songster's faith
　To ask from him a strain of mirth!

No, rather let the murmuring rill
　A low, sweet dirge for Summer sing,
The self-same voice, unchanging still,
　We heard amid the joys of Spring;
When everywhere was glad good-will
　That made the earth with music ring.

The gray clouds flit across the sky,
　And pass their shadows o'er the ground;
October's wind sweeps sadly by,
　A hollow murmur in its sound;
We sadden when the flowers die,
　When frost its ruin scatters round.

Ah! soon the naked trees shall rear
   Their branches bare against the sky;
And, later, on the hillsides drear,
   The pure white snow in drifts shall lie;
What wonder, then, that Nature here,
   In sorrow mourns, she scarce knows why?

But still thou hast delightful days,
   Serenely calm and bright as well;
October! oh, what words of praise,
   Can all thy hazy beauty tell?
The charm that lingers round our ways,
   That seems on field and wood to dwell.

The Indian Summer glorifies
   The Autumn landscape, far and near;
On distant hills a light mist lies
   That softens all their outline clear.
Such days as these we learn to prize,
   On threshold of the winter drear.

And though sharp frosts have mischief wrought,
   On hillside, wood, and open plain,
With health are Autumn breezes fraught,
   The cool, bright days have come again.
The passing years this truth have taught—
   Each month brings blessings in its train.

October, let thy hand be laid
As light as air on fields of green !
Though leaf and flower and stalk and blade,
Escape not touch of hoar-frost keen,
Let Autumn's breath on hill and glade
Blow lightly, 'neath thy sky serene !

VIII.
THE PARTING WORD.

THE PARTING WORD.

The time has come to part, dear friends,
   Though still there may be much to tell;
No path, however long, but ends;
   Who tarries not too late, does well.

Some sense I have, perhaps, conveyed,
   Some glimpse of man's true destiny,
Some hearts have touched, perchance, and made
   Familiar what is dear to me.

By paths we knew not, sometimes led—
   Another way, perhaps, our choice—
We find that we are comforted,
   And at the end our souls rejoice.

The end for which I strove, is near,
   My plain and simple words are done;
If they but wake an echo clear,
   Reward sufficient have I won.

Who does his duty all the day,
    When comes the night, from toil may cease ;
None takes his recompense away—
    He rests at last in perfect peace.

Though much, perchance, remains to tell
    Of Nature's glories, Love Divine,
The time has come to say " Farewell!"
    And so, the parting word be mine.

NOTES.

An earnest voice in solemn prayer.—Page 26.

The speaker referred to was Phœbe W. Foulke, who, at the time this poem was written, resided at Gwynedd, and frequently appeared in the ministry. The stanza following is a paraphrase of a prayer by her to which the writer listened. The vicinity is remarkable for its beauty of landscape, being exceeded, perhaps, by few localities in this country in that respect. Gwynedd is one of the oldest Friends' meetings in Pennsylvania, having been established in 1698. The present building, a reproduction of which, from a photograph, faces page 25, was erected in 1823. The meeting has fallen off considerably in numbers the past twenty years, many Friends from the vicinity having removed to Norristown or to other places. A large gathering usually assembles in the old meeting-house in late summer when one of the sessions of Abington Quarterly Meeting is held here. Gwynedd was settled by Welsh Friends, whose descendants still people the vicinity.

The horse-block shown in the picture is a relic of antiquity, being probably nearly two centuries old. Formerly women as well as men rode to meeting on horseback, and these blocks, still found at old places of worship, were for their convenience in mounting and dismounting.

In the corner of the graveyard nearest to the southwest end of the meeting-house, many American soldiers were buried during the Revolutionary war, according to tradition. After the battle of Germantown, the meeting-house was used for a time as a hospital for sick and wounded Americans, a number of whom died. The venerable sexton, Hugh Foreman, who is one of the figures shown in the picture, informs me that he has recently dug graves in this section of the grounds, but found nothing beyond three iron coffin handles, in a tolerably good state of preservation.

Gwynedd meeting-house was for a long time the only place of worship within a radius of several miles, and many ancient associations naturally cluster around the spot.

The Summer sun is smiling down
Upon the hills of Norristown.—Page 41.
(See also fronti-piece.)

Norristown, the county-seat of Montgomery, contained, at the time the county was formed, in 1784, less than a hundred inhabitants. Its situation is hilly, overlooking the Schuylkill river. It was incorporated as a borough in 1812. In 1816 it contained about a hundred dwellings. It is a town of considerable importance from a manufacturing standpoint, although the iron industries are now much neglected. Its population in 1890 was 19,750. Its situation being high, it is regarded as healthy, and its population is largely made up of accessions from all portions of the large and prosperous county. Among the important institutions, in addition to the court house, jail, and other public buildings, are the Hospital for the Insane, Charity Hospital, St. Joseph's Protectory, and others. The picture which forms the frontispiece is from a photograph taken from the observatory on Noble street school, looking toward the southeast. In the distance are seen the court house steeple and those of several churches. The hills in the background are those of the Edge Hill range, several miles down the river.

A small and silent company,
For worship gathered here, are we.—Page 41.

Norristown Friends' meeting-house, a picture of which is opposite page 41, was built in 1851. The meeting was established by Gwynedd Monthly Meeting, which is held there every three months, in alternation with Gwynedd and Plymouth. The influx of Friends from other portions of the county has very much increased the membership of late years. The grounds are extensive, comprising an acre of valuable land at the south corner of Swede and Jacoby streets, which is ornamented with handsome maple and other trees. A portion of the grounds on Jacoby street, in the rear of the meeting-house, was used as a burial-place for some time after the establishment of the meeting, but there have been no interments here for many years, Norristown Friends generally interring their dead at Plymouth burying-ground, four miles distant.

Abington.—Page 69.

Abington meeting-house was erected in 1700. John Barnes, by deed dated Second-month 5, 1697, vested in trustees 120 acres of land for the benefit of a meeting house and the maintenance of a school. Prior to that time the Friends of the vicinity had met at Oxford, now Trinity Church, or at private houses, one location being the residence of Richard Wall, in Cheltenham. Everard Bolton, an ancestor of the author, his daughter Mary having married Edward Roberts in 1714, as the monthly meeting records show, was Treasurer and a very active member of the meeting for many years. Benjamin Lay, the first writer against slavery in this country, was an attendant here, and his remains were interred in the graveyard adjoining. In 1786 the east end of the house was enlarged, and eleven years later the west end, to accommodate the Quarterly Meeting, recently established. The graveyard was enlarged about a half-century ago. The two-hundredth anniversary of the Monthly Meeting was celebrated Twelfth-month 3, 1882. A Friends' school has been maintained here from time immemorial, and for a number of years a Friends' Boarding School, a large building having been erected for the purpose. The grove of oaks which surrounds the meeting-house is one of the finest in this country.

Words Fitly Spoken.—Page 75.

This poem was suggested to the author by a very appropriate letter of condolence sent to him by his friend, Rev. Charles Collins, shortly after the death of his father, Hugh Roberts, which occurred August 23, 1894, at Norristown.

Horsham Meeting-House.—Page 79.

Horsham meeting was established in 1716. Hannah Carpenter donated fifty acres of land. The first meeting-house on the site was completed about 1724. It stood until 1803, when it was torn down and the present structure was erected. The ancient graveyard contains several acres. Abington Quarterly Meeting is held here in Fifth-month of each year.

The Wissahickon.—Page 109.

The picture which faces this page is from a photograph taken just below the bridge on the State road a mile and a quarter west of Gwynedd Meeting. The other picture, opposite page 111, is near Cleaver's mill, several miles lower down the stream. The author has in his possession a small collection of Indian relics, found by him in the vicinity of the spot where the first picture was taken.

To an Oak Tree.—Page 113.

The oak-tree shown in the picture is on the Arch street road, a short distance northeast of the borough line of Norristown.

The Old Schoolhouse.—Page 129.

The illustration shows Chestnut Grove public school in Lower Makefield township, Bucks county, Pa. It is located between Langhorne and Edgewood, being something more than a mile from the last-named village. Here the author was a pupil in 1861-2-3. It was the last educational institution attended by him. The poem describes a visit thirty years or more later.

The Schuylkill sweeps in flashing splendor by.—Page 174.

The photograph was taken from a point near the foot of Buttonwood street, Norristown, looking towards the Valley Forge hills, which appear in the distance. The upper end of Barbadoes island is shown on the left, covered with trees.

The far-off hills it softens,
Their summits glorifies.—Page 178.

This poem, ".A Midsummer Day," is not a mere fancy. It is a description as accurate as the author knew how to make it of a day in late June, 1895. The "river, field and forest" are the Schuylkill above Swede street dam, the west bank of the Schuylkill, and the woods on Fairview Heights, Bridgeport. The "far-off hills" are those of Valley Forge in the distance. The scene presented a most beautiful picture on the day mentioned. It may be added here, what probably the reader has already discovered, that all the other descriptions of natural objects in the volume are taken from reality.

Austin L. Taggart.—Page 242.

Austin L. Taggart, a farmer of Upper Merion, who served four terms in the Pennsylvania Legislature. He was born in Tamaqua, November 21, 1836. His legislative career was characterized by devotion to the interests of his constituents. He opposed the reëlection of Senator Cameron in 1891, becoming a candidate himself for the position, although with no hope of succeeding. He died February 15, 1894, and the lines on page 242 appeared next day in the " Norristown Herald." He was prominent among the Grangers, a Republican in politics, and a representative man in the best sense of the word.

At Rest.—Page 247.

This poem was written immediately after the death of the author's second son, Charles Alfred Roberts, who died March 14, 1888, aged nearly seven years. His last illness, which covered only a few days, included the period of the great storm at that time, commonly known as the "blizzard," to which there is an allusion in the last stanza.

INDEX.

www.ingramcontent.com/pod-product-compliance
Lightning Source LLC
Chambersburg PA
CBHW020943120726
47905CB00008B/2656